To anyone who doesn'ı

The Faker's Guide to Self-Improvement

SHALON ATWOOD

Flower & Vine Press

2025

Chapter 1

Fourteen Years Ago

Valerie Knight slumped against the scratchy hospital pillow, sweat-soaked hair clinging to the back of her neck. The stampede of elephants in her chest finally subsided, and a wave of exhaustion swept over her. Holy shit.

"Did I tear my asshole?" she mumbled to no one in particular.

Seriously, though, had she?

Although logically aware of how difficult this would be on her body, she had not expected her nether regions to feel like they had been seared on a flaming grill. Like a hamburger.

And there had been absolutely nothing to prepare her mentally. What kind of mindfuckery was society playing at here? After decades of medical advances, there had to be a better way. Couldn't humans be grown in pods by now? If she had known how barbaric it all was, would she have willingly endured this torture?

A pterodactyl-like wail pierced the air, and the answer to that question ripped Val's heart straight from her chest. Emotion cascaded over her, threatening to overwhelm her senses and turn her into a blubbering mess. A state Val never found herself in. How was it possible to love someone with such intensity before you even laid eyes on them? She pushed herself up as carefully as she could, ready to take her daughter into her arms.

But before her husband, Peter, could make his way across the room with their newly wrapped infant, the doors of the birthing suite flew open, and Val's mother sauntered in. Dressed in a cream-colored power suit with perfectly coiffed hair and a face so dewy and relaxed, one might think she'd come straight from the spa.

"Did I miss it?" her mother asked with an airy tone, as if she didn't care one way or another. Judging by the way she gripped her purse with

1

just her fingertips, she had probably spent Val's agonizing labor getting her nails done. Which sounded about right.

"Yeah, Mom, you missed it." Val flopped her head back onto the pillow. She didn't have the energy to deal with her mom right now, or ever, come to think of it. What had made Val believe that her mom would show up for her this time? Twenty-six years, and Val still clung to some adolescent hope that she would be the priority, just this once.

What she had needed was a hand to hold and someone to tell her everything would be okay. Instead, she had Peter, a man with no reference point for childbirth, telling her how to breathe from her diaphragm and to "just ride the wave" whenever a contraction hit.

She wanted Peter to ride that wave straight out to the middle of the ocean, never to be seen again.

"Oh, you're right on time," Peter said. The traitorous bastard.

With his attention on the bundle in his hands, he crossed the room toward her mother while Val mentally kicked him in the shin.

"Lucy, meet your granddaughter, Layla," he said, cradling the baby's head toward her. "Congratulations, Grandma."

Her mom scoffed, took a step back, and placed a perfectly manicured hand on her chest, clearly offended. "*Grandma* makes me sound so old." She grimaced. "This little one can just call me Lulu."

Ugh. She can't be serious. Lulu was the nickname of a little girl, not a grandmother. She could have gone with Nana, Bubbe, Nonna, Gran, she didn't have to pick Grandma. But Lulu? Sure, objectively better than Memaw, but still.

Her mom set her purse on a nearby chair and stretched an arm out, a finger reaching toward the baby's face. A finger that had just come from the salon and who knows where else? A finger that hadn't been scrubbed with soap or sanitizer. A finger that would rub all the world's outside germs on her precious baby's face if she didn't do something.

"Mom, stop!" Val said, bolting upright in bed. Her mistake was immediately evident.

Blinding heat shot through her as the raw meat between her legs chafed against the rough bedsheet, lighting her entire body on fire. Spots danced in her vision, and she struggled to formulate words.

It was as if she had taken steel wool to scratch off yet another layer of skin from her crotch. Someone just knock her out already.

When the world finally righted itself and she could breathe again, she leaned to the side and rested her body weight on one ass cheek. She sucked in air and did her best to ignore the throbbing pain that had made it all the way up to her eyeballs. How was she supposed to survive off one extra-strength ibuprofen after all this?

"Oh, Valerie, she's beautiful," her mother cooed.

Val opened her eyes to see her mother cradling Layla in her arms, and to her horror, poking at her beautiful face with that dirty finger.

"Mom!" she said, drawing the word out like a sullen teenager who hadn't gotten her way. She couldn't help it. There was just something about her mom that brought out the worst in her.

"Did you say something, honey?" her mother said as she rubbed the next mass contagion all over Layla's face.

"You have to wash your hands before you touch a newborn. Everyone knows that." At least, any reasonable, responsible parent would.

"Psh." Her mom waved away her concern, continuing to stroke Layla's cheek as if Val had said nothing.

Because why would she start listening now?

Chapter 2

Present Day

Hunched over her office desk with her head in her hands, Val held in an exasperated groan. This was the second time this week the nursing home needed her for some emergency or another. She paid them an exorbitant amount of money, didn't she? Couldn't they handle it?

She kept her voice low so as not to draw attention from the rest of the staff. Sharing the bullpen with fifteen other writers for *Mile High Magazine* meant that conversations were never private, but Val needed this one to be.

"I have a deadline to meet, I can't just drop everything to talk my mother off a ledge." Never mind that the deadline had already passed, and she was nowhere near finished. But she would be if they would just stop calling her.

Val ran a finger along her eyebrow to smooth out the wrinkle that had been getting deeper since her mother's dementia started barreling toward oncoming traffic. Her face had been set to a perpetual scowl for the last month, the vise grip of her jaw grinding the enamel off her molars, her daily ibuprofen barely keeping the migraines at bay. Couldn't they just keep her mother sedated? Hell, she wouldn't mind being sedated herself.

Her computer pinged, drawing her attention to a new email notification with a subject that read: *Enjoy These Birthday Savings, You Deserve It!* She slammed her laptop shut. Why had she ever given out her real birthday? This reminder wasn't needed; she'd prefer to forget entirely. Especially a birthday that held such significance. Forty was a milestone, as they say.

Yeah, a decade closer to death.

The nurse's deep, sympathetic voice over the phone brought her back to the present. "Look, I understand that this is hard for you, but you know what your mother is like."

And Val got it. At the end of the day, he had other shit to do, too. Dealing with confused old lady tantrums was above his pay grade.

"I know, I know. I'll be there in twenty." She hung up the phone and craned her neck over the cubicle wall she shared with Maddie, but her chair sat empty. Good, maybe Val could sneak out of here just one time without some massive guilt trip from the brown-noser.

Val had once heard someone refer to Maddie as the golden retriever of the office, presumably because she was kind, reliable, and friends with everyone. But Val thought of her more as a stray dog, always in search of validation, with this incessant need to be convinced of what a great job she was doing. Whereas Val did her best to project Doberman Pinscher vibes: confident, aloof, stay-out-of-my-way-or-I-will-bite-your-face-off sort of energy.

For the most part, it worked. Val was left alone to do her job, which was how she liked it. But for some reason, Maddie could never take the hint, always tossing her sugary sweet greetings, inviting her to the office happy hours and nosing into her business like they were besties.

Val stuffed her laptop in her bag, slung it over her shoulder, and walked toward the hall as if it were completely normal to cut out of the office just ten minutes before an incredibly important meeting.

"Hey, Val!" Maddie said as she stepped out of the elevator, two coffees in hand. No more than thirty years old, ridiculously tall with a bony frame, and a dark brown pixie cut, Maddie was a walking stick figure. She could blow over in the slightest breeze.

"I picked up coffee for you," she said, holding out the cup. "Black, like your soul." Maddie giggled at her own joke.

Val sighed and took the cup, offering Maddie a tight smile. "Thanks."

Maddie's shoulders hunched. "Oh, I'm sorry, I didn't even ask you first. Maybe you wanted something else or—"

Val held up a hand to stop her. "Maddie, it's fine."

In Maddie's quest to people-please, she had a habit of apologizing for any minor inconvenience, particularly those that weren't her fault, and Val just couldn't deal with that right now.

"Thank you." Val held up the coffee and nodded in Maddie's direction before punching the elevator button. She sent up a silent plea to the gods of Minding One's Own Business that this would be the end of their conversation.

"You're not leaving, are you?" Maddie said, her voice laced with concern. "The meeting's about to start."

Of course the gods hadn't listened, when did they ever? Val sucked in a deep breath and adjusted her face from the death glare she was probably giving to soft puppy dog eyes that could possibly garner some sympathy. It felt weird.

"Oh, Mad, something's come up, and I've gotta jet. Can you cover for me?"

Maddie's eyebrows shot to her hairline. "Val, no!" she hissed. "You're already on thin ice. I covered for you last time and the time before that." Her hands jerked as she spoke, the coffee in her cup sloshing out the top. "You haven't even turned in your article yet!"

Val cringed. Yes, the article had been due last week, but Val would get it done, she always did. Besides, she didn't have to answer to Maddie.

"What is so important that you need to run out again?" Maddie threw a hand on her hip, judgment spewing from her eyeballs. And for a moment, Val thought maybe she got Maddie all wrong. She wasn't a golden retriever, she was one of those small dogs that continuously bark at your feet, threatening to trip you up if you're not careful. Which was to say: annoying as hell.

Val struggled for an excuse. No one at work knew about her mother's illness. In fact, they thought her mother was dead. Why? She told them so. She recalled all the cards and flowers that showed up on her desk the week that she requested bereavement leave to attend her mother's funeral, when all she was doing was helping move her mom into the care facility and selling her house. Honestly, though, her mother had been dead to her for years, so what difference did it make?

Besides, she didn't want to be buddy-buddy with anyone here, so why did they need to know anything about her? At the office, she simply wanted to be known as Valerie Knight: investigative journalist. Not divorced single mom with a mother who didn't remember who she was. If Layla hadn't insisted on coming to that "take your daughter to work day" a few years ago, no one would even know she had a kid.

"Family emergency," Val said as she punched the button again and cursed the four flights of stairs she would most certainly have to hoof down if the elevator didn't arrive soon.

"Is Layla okay?" Maddie's mood shifted from suspicion to concern, and while Val should feel guilty for lying, she absolutely didn't.

"She just got her period at school, and I need to take her a change of clothes, you know?" The elevator dinged, saving her from having to say more.

Maddie nodded. "Well, you better hurry. I'll do my best to cover for you, but I don't know what Sonia will do if you don't show up at all."

Val couldn't imagine her boss actually doing anything. She might be *eternally disappointed* in her, a phrase Val had heard on numerous occasions, but would she do something about it? Val had her doubts.

"Thank you, Mad, you're the best!" The smile Val had plastered on fell the minute the doors closed.

• • • •

THE EARLY MAY SUN HAD already reached near blinding levels by the time Val pulled her car out of the parking garage, and of course, she left her sunglasses in the office. She cursed, adjusting the visor to block out as much of the glare as she could. The Colorado sun was a bright constant, beaming straight into her corneas regardless of the time of year. While most Boulder residents delighted in the cloudless skies, Val often wanted to chuck that ball of cheer straight into a black hole.

She squinted for the entire five miles of the drive to the nursing home, her wrinkles sinking deeper into her skull. Great, if this visit didn't give her a migraine, the sun certainly would.

The staff of the memory care unit at Foothills Village were in a tizzy by the time Val made it inside. They dashed from one room to the next, their ID cards swinging from their belts. Even from all the way down the hall, Val could hear aggravated shouts coming from her mother's room, no doubt setting off other residents into panic mode.

It figured, her mother had always been a bit of a drama queen. An attention whore. Why would any of that change now?

Val trudged down the hall. Even the threat of missing the staff meeting couldn't get her to pick up her feet.

She hated this place. Impossibly beige walls adorned with the occasional piece of dull, boring landscape. Everything was void of color.

The low lighting and classical music tinkling from the speakers were most likely intended to keep an air of pleasant calm, but it just reminded Val of riding an elevator with a stranger: tight smiles, avoiding eye contact, neither party wanting to be there.

Val fanned the collar of her shirt, desperate for a crank in the AC, the faint scent of urine in the air turning her stomach.

How could a place so insanely expensive be as equally depressing?

Another shout and the sound of glass shattering quickened Val's pace to a jog. Not again. Hadn't she cleared her room of all breakables the last time this happened? She passed an older man holding his ears and facing the wall, a staff member leaning over, whispering words of assurance in his ear, and she couldn't help but feel annoyed at her mother. For making everything about her. As always.

By the time Val made it to her mother's room, a staff member was on their knees, sweeping up what looked to be a broken vase, while another restrained her mother's hands. God, this woman. Always resorting to dramatics.

Her mother sat hunched in her wheelchair, her back rounded like her spine had completely given up. Silver wisps of hair barely covered her scalp, unlike the thick dark curls she sported in her younger days.

"Oh!" Her mother's demeanor shifted at the sight of Val, her face lighting up like she might actually recognize her this time. And finally be happy to see her.

"Hi, Mom," Val said, throwing apologetic smiles to the staff as she made her way across the room.

"Could you tell them?" her mother pleaded. "I need to find it!" Panic filled her mom's eyes, and even though doing *this* and being *here* was the last thing Val needed right now, something tugged at her heart.

Val knelt beside her mother's chair and held her hand. "What, Mom? What do you need to find?"

"My daughter," she said, patting Val's arm. "It's her birthday today, and I can't find her present. I just know it's here somewhere."

Val's heart leaped at the prospect of her mother remembering her birthday. Maybe it would be a good day, after all.

"It's okay." The paper-thin skin of her mom's hand felt extra fragile, like Val might tear right through it if she wasn't careful.

"She's thirteen," her mom continued. "She'll be so sad if I miss her birthday."

And just like that, Val's heart sagged, and her defenses rose.

If memory had served, her mom missed her thirteenth birthday. Val had sat in that Mexican restaurant eating free chips and salsa for an hour until the staff took pity on her and brought out the dessert. There had been nothing more humiliating than eating fried ice cream all by herself on the day she officially became a teenager.

"Well, it wouldn't be the first time you missed my birthday," Val muttered, failing to keep the annoyance out of her voice, her knees cracking as she stood.

"Oh, dear," her mom said, bringing her trembling hands to her face.

It had been the wrong thing to say, but Val couldn't help it. She was always tripping up when she came to visit, the staff usually correcting her behavior or word choice, constantly reminding her that she was a terrible person. Sure, they were nice about it, but they had to know that Val hadn't signed up for this. She hadn't signed up to coddle and soothe this shell of a person who never exhibited any compassion herself.

"Where is it?" Her mother's voice cracked, and Val could sense the tension building in her. They were moments away from her losing it. Again.

Val sighed and sat back down. She wasn't getting out of here anytime soon.

"Hey, how about I just sit here with you for a bit, huh?" Val rubbed slow circles on her mom's back, fingers running over the sharp points of her shoulder blades.

The orderly dumped the broken glass into a garbage can and tossed Val a relieved smile before leaving the room. Val's gaze followed him out and snagged on a vase of fresh-cut flowers on the counter. Who brought those? Val was the only visitor her mom had. Maybe they had been left in the wrong room. Or more likely, a florist donated their leftovers to brighten up the place. Either way, they needed to go into a plastic cup before she left. She wouldn't want that vase to get hurled at a person's head next time.

While her mom still buzzed with agitation beside her, Val kept up her slow circles and contemplated what to make for dinner because she might as well get something done if she was going to be stuck here. She made a mental list of the contents of their refrigerator: shredded chicken left over from taco night, eggs, a wrinkly pepper, and a bag of baby carrots. Maybe it was time for a stir-fry. Or she could stop by her favorite Thai place after work for some take-out. What would Layla be in the mood for?

Her mom's hand on hers broke her out of her thoughts. Thin, cold fingers patted Val's gently, signaling that things were all right now. This was really all it took, just being here for a few minutes until the tension and anxiety abated, and then her mom would settle. Still confused, not really there, but settled enough to not take out her frustration on the ceramics.

Val sneaked a glance at her watch. The staff meeting was well underway, and Val would never hear the end of it. But as long as she turned her article in by the end of the day, Sonia would forgive her. Right?

Chapter 3

"Val, I'd like to see you, please." Sonia ducked her head back into her office, not even giving Val the chance to set her stuff down.

"What, does she have a tracker on my shoe or something?" Val mumbled to herself.

She had been in the building for less than thirty seconds and wasn't sure she had any energy left to hear another disappointed speech from her boss. While Val could never be considered a vast well of patience and empathy, what little hid in her bones had been sucked out by her mother. She was an empty husk.

Sonia steepled her fingers and sighed. "Listen, Val. You haven't met a deadline in months, and you're barely at your desk." She leaned back in her chair and crossed her arms over her chest.

Val did her best to look contrite. Sonia wasn't wrong, after all. "I know. The last few months have been challenging for me if I'm being honest."

Sonia raised her eyebrows as if expecting Val to continue. But what could she say? She couldn't tell Sonia the truth—that she had skipped out on work countless times because her mother was a bag of bones with a feisty temper. For all Sonia knew, her mother had been dead for a year. *Surprise, I lied!* No, Val couldn't come back from that one.

"It's just..." Val's mind raced with excuses, but for once, she came up empty.

"That's what I thought." Sonia slapped her hand on the desk. "I'm afraid I have to give your column over to Cari."

"What?" Val spluttered. "*Cokehead* Cari? You're not serious!"

Taking her column away was one thing, but giving it to that strung-out chatterbox was a real titty twister. What would she write about anyway? Her next tummy tuck? A listicle of conspiracy theories she ascribed to?

Sonia's face held an unreadable expression, and she said nothing.

"So you're demoting me. Fine, I'll—"

"No, Val. You're fired."

Val scrunched her face and shook her head because there was no way she heard that right.

"Listen, I'm sorry I missed the meeting, I just had to step out for a moment. It won't happen again, I swear!"

Sonia held up a hand to stop her. "It's not just today, and you know it."

Being fired wasn't an option. Who was going to keep her lights on or pay the unholy monthly fees for her mom's care?

"Sonia," she said, her voice pleading, "I always come through for you."

And for a moment, Val was positive she had her. Sonia sighed and nodded. Because it was true. Sure, she'd rather jab a pencil in her eye than attend a staff meeting, and yeah, she'd missed a deadline or two. But she always got her work done. Sometimes she just needed a couple more days to really get inspired. And she could barely do that around the office dickwads. And her mom's tantrums certainly didn't help.

"You can submit articles on a freelance basis, but there's no guarantee that I'll publish them."

Val shuddered. Instead of being a full-time content writer, she was now a dreaded freelancer. She hadn't worked her ass off for this long to not know when she was getting paid next. She had too many bills for that uncertainty.

Trying another tactic, Val attempted another round of puppy dog eyes and pleaded. Right now, she would beg, grovel, whatever it took to continue receiving a regular paycheck.

"Sonia, please don't fire me."

• • • •

VAL HEAVED HER BODY against the double doors, a guttural roar escaping from deep inside her chest. Her pulse throbbed in her ears, and her skin burned from the humiliation of it all.

She juggled the box of personal effects in her hand as she spun around to kick the door for good measure. But before she had the chance, Maddie swung it open, no doubt to lay on an *I told you so*.

"Yeah, yeah, yeah," Val spat. "I know. I should have listened to you."

Maddie reached out as if to touch her arm, but Val jerked away before she got a chance.

"I'm so sorry, Val," Maddie said, like it was her fault.

"Forget it." Val heaved a sigh and turned toward the pedestrian mall.

"Oh, wait," Maddie called from the doorway. "You forgot your phone."

Val swiped the phone from Maddie's hand and shoved it into her back pocket.

"Look on the bright side," Maddie said with a pitying smile on her face. "You hated coming into the office. And now you don't have to."

Of course Maddie was the silver lining type of asshole.

Val squinted up at the brick building where she started her writing career. The hours she spent researching and agonizing over articles, reporting on local issues that mattered. Increased fracking, wildfire devastation, and the battle against a small band of local conspiracy theorists who were desperate to teach school children that Earth was flat. Had it been her favorite stuff to write? No, but at least it meant a steady paycheck.

She balanced the box in one hand and raised a middle finger to the top floor just in case anyone might see her from the conference room.

"It'll be okay," said Maddie and her toxic positivity. "You'll find something else, I'm sure of it."

If Val had been larger than 5'5" with any sort of muscles, she would have picked Maddie up like the freaking pencil she was, spun her around over her head, and hurled her straight into the burning sun.

Ignoring her calls of sympathy, Val left Maddie on the corner and stomped across the street. She needed to make a plan. A money-making plan. She had bills to pay and a teenager with a newly acquired taste for designer jeans, who wouldn't quit growing.

Her butt vibrated. She pulled her phone from her back pocket and crossed her fingers it would be Sonia. Calling to take it all back, to return the column to its rightful owner. But it wasn't Sonia. It was her ex-husband, Peter. Val growled at her phone. Why hadn't he returned her call two days ago when she actually wanted to talk to him?

"What the hell, Peter?" She certainly wasn't in the mood for pleasantries, but her ragey tone surprised even her. It usually took them a few verbal volleys before she reached this level of aggravation.

A classic Peter sigh came from the other end of the line. The long, deep exhale you might hear in a yoga class. What was it called again? Oh, right. Ocean's breath. She hated that she knew that, but she had lived with him and his meditating ass for far too long.

"Happy birthday, Val!" Of course he completely ignored her outburst; he probably anticipated it.

"Oh, fuck off."

"I'm just calling you back. No need to get up in arms." His voice was calm and measured.

She could picture him on his yoga mat, his phone in speaker-mode on the coffee table. Was he in tree pose, perhaps? Yes. Standing on one leg, hands together in prayer, breathing like the freaking ocean. What she would give to be there and kick that goddamn leg out from under him.

"I called you two days ago. What if this was an emergency?"

"So it's not an emergency. What is it?" His voice was casual and nonchalant and annoying as hell. She gritted her teeth.

Talking to Peter was a lot like being on a battlefield. Val had her weapons handy, ready to cut him down over the phone. They had only been divorced for a little over a year, but they fought like this for most of their marriage. With all the practice, she had become an expert wielder of the spoken sword.

"Do you have any idea what Layla was doing when she was with you this weekend? Do you?" Val was shouting, but the pedestrian mall was mostly empty, and so what? Let the tourists think she was a busker putting on a show. Hell, she could use the money now.

"She went to her friend's house, Val, it's no big deal. You let her have sleepovers, too." His tone was finally prickly, as if his yoga breath no longer served him. Good.

Val huffed and drew her imaginary sword. She had to keep herself from screaming at the top of her lungs, "I don't let our daughter sleep over with *criminals*!"

During the beat of silence that followed, a triumphant wave of pride washed over her. She might officially be unemployed, but she would finally score one in the better parent column.

"Wha...what do you mean?"

"Daisy's brother. He was just released from jail." Blade against his neck.

"Ah. You mean the wilderness program for at-risk teens?" And just like that, her sword went flying, clattering to the concrete. How did he know that?

"He assaulted someone!" Val was near hysterics now, desperate for a win.

They say that smiles can be heard through the phone, and it wasn't until this very moment that Val could vouch for that. Peter had to have been grinning from ear to ear based on his condescending and smug tone.

"Underage weed possession," he said, winning yet another round.

Goddamn it! Val stomped her foot.

"Look, I know that she just turned fourteen," he continued. "She has a lifetime of pot smoking ahead of her, and it doesn't need to start right now."

Exactly what she had been thinking. How did he always do that? Throw her own thoughts back in her face?

"Right!" Val said. "So she doesn't need to be around it at all!"

"She's a good kid, you have to start trusting her."

Before Val could say anything or chuck her phone into the nearby fountain, Peter continued, his voice softer this time. "Hey, how's your mom doing?"

Her feet stopped moving. She leaned against a short iron fence, her heart now up in her throat. The sun beat down on her vintage T-shirt, and she cursed herself for wearing black today. Sweat beaded on the back of her neck, and she pulled at her collar. Why was it so hot? It was barely summer.

"Val?" Peter said softly. "You know I'm here if you ever need to talk."

Val couldn't hang up fast enough. She didn't need Peter feeling sorry for her or checking in on her. Not today, not ever. Why did he care anyway? He wasn't her husband or even a friend anymore. They were, at best, two people who yelled at each other on a semi-regular basis. And what would she talk about? How she had just been fired and could no longer afford her mother's care?

As the reality of her situation settled in, a nerve behind her eye throbbed, and she rested her back against the fence, dropping the box to the ground. What was she going to do now? What was she going to tell Layla? Her heart twisted at the thought of her daughter, and her eyes stung with something hot and angry. Christ, was she going to cry out here in the middle of the pedestrian mall? She shoved her phone into her back pocket, blinking fast.

A picture of Peter popped into her head again with his impeccable posture and long brown hair pulled back into a ponytail, offering to pay her bills until she got back on her feet. Because that was something he would do.

"Oh, go fuck yourself!" she mumbled to this image of him.

At least, she had meant to mumble.

"Someone forgot to take her meds this morning," said a low voice from behind her.

Val stiffened at the dig and slowly turned to find the source of the insult. Three college-aged boys sat inside the fence, decked out in their CU Boulder T-shirts, their meaty shoulders giving off massive gym-bro vibes. One of them chomped into the biggest burrito Val had ever seen, sauce dribbling down his chin.

"You lost?" The speaker of the group had a chiseled face and bleach blond hair; he would probably be at home on a set of *Baywatch*.

They all snickered. Val's blood pressure began to rise, and a roaring filled her ears like a wave coming up to crush her skull. Or that migraine finally settling in. She had dealt with enough shit today, she didn't need to put up with this asshole.

"What did you say?" she said, her hands balled into fists at her sides.

They continued to laugh and smack one another on the shoulder, like riling up a strange woman on the street was the highlight of their day. These were clearly some trust fund kids whose parents bought their way into college. They certainly weren't there for their intellect.

"Go take your meds, you crazy bitch," Baywatch boy said, confirming her suspicions. He leaned over the fence and shooed her away with a flick of his hand.

Without another thought, Val shot her right arm out like a rocket, aiming directly for his perfect nose. The heel of her hand connected with his face with such force, the initial smack of skin and subsequent pop of cartilage was a sound she delighted in for weeks to come.

The guy jumped to his feet and cradled his nose, blood gushing between his fingers.

"What the hell?" His pronouncement garbled.

This would be the point where any sane person took a step back and assessed what had just occurred. Apologize, get some tissues, pull out some cash to slap on the table for their trouble, and haul ass out of there.

Val, however, was not a normal person today. She was a pot of fury and frustration that had been set to simmer for far too long. She was finally boiling over.

Taking advantage of his hunched position, she rammed her elbow into his stomach, which caused him to topple backward, trip on a chair behind him, and send his tall body crashing to the ground. She propped her hands on the iron fence that stood between him and the swift kick to the dick she had every intent on delivering, but before she could move another inch, a shout pierced the air.

"Mom!"

Val swung her head in the direction of Layla's shocked voice, and there she stood, flanked by a group of wide-eyed teenagers, who were probably thanking the stars that it wasn't their mother acting completely nuts in public. And because the sight of her daughter always brightened her day, even when Layla was being a complete shit, Val couldn't help but smile and wave, just as a pair of meaty hands circled her body and hauled her backward off the fence.

"Layla!" she cried as Baywatch boy's friend immobilized her.

A small crowd had gathered during the kerfuffle, phones snapping pictures, someone surely calling the police. She scanned the faces until she caught sight of the back of Layla's head, scurrying away from the disaster that was her mother. And why wouldn't she run away from this spectacle? Val had lost her mind and didn't have the decency to do it in private.

With her arms pinned to her sides, Val could do nothing but sag against the rock-hard muscle that held her. Which was fine with her.

That had been more exercise than she had gotten in weeks, and she was exhausted.

And she still hadn't figured out what to make for dinner.

Chapter 4

"Wow, leave it to Boulder to punish you by making you talk about your feelings," Layla said as they trekked down the steps of the courthouse three months later.

Bringing Layla to her sentencing hadn't been Val's idea, but Peter thought it would be educational for her to see how a courtroom operated. And listening to Val read her apology letter (however contrived it had been) might help in convincing Layla that Val wasn't a complete shitshow. It didn't work.

"Hey, I'll take a court-ordered therapist over jail time any day."

Although, talking about her feelings with a stranger was not appealing in the least. And paying for it out of pocket was going to be brutal; her credit cards were already reaching their limits. But even she had to admit it was the best-case scenario. Although there was a tiny part of her that couldn't help but wonder how much writing she might get done in a quiet jail cell. All alone. Just her and her thoughts.

Okay, yes, therapy was the way to go here.

Intense July heat radiated off the concrete, a drastic change from the over-air-conditioned building they were just in.

Val pulled her hair back into a ponytail and wiggled out of her blazer, letting it hang from her purse straps. "Damn, it's hot out here!"

"Oh, but, Mom," Layla said in her best pretentious voice, "at least it's a *dry* heat."

Val swatted at her. "Stop it! Ninety-five degrees is ninety-five degrees!" She shook her fists in the air. "I'm going to slap the next person that says that to me."

Layla snorted. "And then I think you'd finally end up in jail."

Val stopped on the sidewalk and turned to Layla. "Do you think I deserved jail time?"

"You broke that guy's nose!" Layla said with more than a touch of incredulity, pulling her long-sleeved shirt over her head and tying it

23

around her waist. She clipped her cross-body bag over her black tank and kept walking.

Val scurried to catch up. "I know, and I'm sorry you saw that. I truly didn't know you'd be off campus for lunch."

Layla scoffed. "That's why you're sorry? Because I saw it?"

"No! Of course not!" And despite her best efforts, Val's voice rose an octave as she said those words. She cleared her throat and tried again. "Listen. That was a rough day for me, and apparently, the judge agreed."

"And being a middle-aged white woman had nothing to do with it?"

Damn this generation and their awareness! It was mind-boggling sometimes.

"No, you're absolutely right. I sometimes forget how perceptive you are." Layla cast a look over her shoulder like she didn't buy that at all, so Val hastily added, "And how unfair our judicial system is." This earned Val an approving nod. "But you didn't actually want me to go to jail, did you?"

Drawing on the power of teenage angst, Layla rolled her beautiful brown eyes as far back in her head as she could get them. One of these times, she was going to roll those little gooey balls so hard, her brain would suck them in, and she would be left with gaping sockets.

"Oh, so I could go stay with Dad and get out from under your constant surveillance? Gee, of course not."

It was Val's turn to roll her eyes. "And then we would miss out on so much mother-daughter bonding." Val nudged Layla with her hip, checking her face for any hint of a smile. Nothing.

Like everyone else in the world, Layla had a couple of inches on Val, so when Val slung an arm over her shoulder and pulled her in for a side hug, Layla's long brown curls brushed Val's cheek. The scent of her floral shampoo wafted off her and made Val long for the days when she could dive her nose into her baby's hair, and it wouldn't be weird.

Staying at home with a newborn had been stressful and some of the most challenging days Val had ever experienced. But there had been nothing better than Layla fast asleep on her chest. Val would nuzzle Layla's head right under her chin and breathe in her scent for hours.

As if sensing some motherly nostalgia, Layla pushed her away. She took a pair of sunglasses out of her bag and popped them onto her face. They made her appear older than her fourteen years. And with the streak of blue running through her hair, she was definitely a lot cooler than Val had ever been.

"And you consider taking me to your court appearance a 'bonding moment'?" Layla's voice dripped with sarcasm, which was clearly a gift from Val, so she couldn't be mad about it.

"Of course not! But I'm taking you back-to-school shopping. That's bonding, right? And then tonight we'll order some celebratory pizza. Pizza that says, 'my mom is going to therapy and not jail.'" Val gave Layla her best jazz hands.

"God, Mom!"

Once on the road, Val pushed her sunglasses onto her nose and flipped the visor down to block just a little of the extreme glare from the sun. It was like an intense flashlight aimed straight into her pupils. How thousands of people drove around in this every day without crashing into one another was a miracle.

Shoving aside all thoughts of her very empty bank account, she made a mental list of everything they would need to buy: socks, underwear, shoes. Everything else could wait or be thrifted. She certainly wasn't going to fork over eighty dollars on whatever pair of jeans happened to be in these days.

"How are you on bras, honey? I can't remember the last time I bought you some."

"Ugh." Layla crossed her arms and slumped down into the seat. "Just give me your credit card, and I'll get what I need."

Val barked out a laugh. "Not a chance in hell."

"Daisy has her own credit card. She isn't forced to buy bras with her mom."

"We're all forced to buy bras with our moms. It's just how it's done." Val could recall the one and only time her mom took her shopping for underwear. Only, her mom had parked herself at the makeup counter and handed Val a twenty-dollar bill. *Knock yourself out* was all she had said. Maybe if her mom had cared to advise her in any way, Val wouldn't have worn pinchy, ill-fitting undergarments for an entire decade. She was determined for Layla to have a better experience.

"Besides," Val continued, "we're not swimming in money like Daisy's family."

If not for the unemployment checks, Val would have had to disconnect their Wi-Fi weeks ago. And based on her calculations, she only had a couple of months left before their financial situation would become dire. Submitting freelance articles was proving fruitless thus far, though she wasn't giving up. If only she could somehow get her column back.

"Would you rather go bra shopping with your dad?" Val glanced over, hoping to catch a smile.

Instead, Layla hunched near the passenger door, her face glowing from a phone screen. But it didn't look like Layla's phone. No, it most certainly wasn't Layla's phone. What the hell?

With her attention still on the road, Val reached over and tore the phone from Layla's hand.

"Mom!"

"Are you shitting me? Is this an iPhone?" Val turned it over, and sure enough, the Apple logo stared back at her. It was the one thing Peter and Val had decided long ago never to give their child. What teenager needed a phone so expensive?

"Language, Mom, god." Layla snatched the phone back and tucked it into her pocket. She slouched into the seat.

"And since when do you have an iPhone?"

"Dad got it for me. For my birthday."

Of course he did. Just to piss Val off, no doubt. "I can't believe that man!" Couldn't he have consulted her first?

"Just drop me off at PF Chang's," Layla said as if Val was her Uber driver.

"You have lunch money for PF Chang's? Because I don't." Great. This was what they got for living in Boulder, where some of Layla's classmates lived in multi-million dollar homes at the base of the foothills and spent their winters skiing in Aspen. And lunching at PF Chang's, apparently.

"I'm not eating here, I'm just meeting people." Layla tucked the blue strand of hair behind her ear and crossed her arms over her chest.

"People?" Val imagined a group of juvenile delinquents huddled near the movie theater entrance, ready to knock the shopping bags out of the hands of old ladies.

"I'm meeting friends, okay? Why do you have to be so nosy?"

"Layla, I'm your mother. That's literally my job. Bad things happen to kids without nosy moms. I'm nosy because I care." Val maneuvered her beat-up Honda Civic into the parking lot of Flatirons Mall and headed to the PF Chang's entrance.

"Okay, fine." Val sighed and reached over to...what? Pat Layla like a dog? Pinch her cheeks? She wasn't three anymore. It was hard to know what to do now that Layla was a teen. She pulled her arm back and placed it on the steering wheel. "You're meeting friends. That's fine. But you are not to leave the mall, and I need you back here in one hour. Got it?"

Layla was out of the car before she was done speaking.

"Okay," Val said as the door slammed. "So Mickey Mouse undies then?"

• • • •

"I CAN'T BELIEVE YOU bought her that without consulting me first." Val balanced the phone between her ear and shoulder while flipping through a rack of bralettes, finally understanding why people walked around blaring their phone conversations on speaker. Multitasking was brutal on the neck. "We said we would never get her an iPhone, it's too expensive. I give that screen no more than a month."

Peter's sigh crackled down the line. "I know, but she was due for an upgrade, and this one isn't new. It's refurbished, so not a big deal. And we can track her a bit better on this one."

Tracking their daughter was a fantastic idea, but Val would never admit that to Peter.

"Why do you need to track her? Are you telling me that you don't know where she is when she's with you? Is that what I'm hearing?"

He ignored her tone as he often did. "She's a good kid. Tracking her phone is just for our peace of mind, not for stalking."

Val took a deep breath. He was right. Damn, she hated when Peter was right. "Fine. But you should have talked to me first."

"I know, I'm sorry." Peter sighed. There was a beat of silence before he continued. "So court went okay today?"

She stopped flicking through the bras and took her phone out from the crook of her neck. Rolling her head from side to side to stretch her muscles, she said, "Could have been worse. They're punishing me with therapy."

"That sounds like appropriate punishment. Add in some mandated yoga, and there's your personal hell, right?" Peter's laugh was breathy and good-natured, the kind of laugh that transported her back to their good times. When laughter came easy and they didn't take themselves so seriously. Her heart twisted. But then Peter opened his big mouth again, and she hardened back up.

"Listen," he said, his tone suddenly parental, "I know that money's tight and—"

"Nope," Val said, cutting him off. She didn't need him to swoop down and rescue her from the dumpster fire of her life. A fire she set herself, no less.

She spotted Layla out of the corner of her eye, leaning over the checkout counter, laughing.

With a boy.

The sight almost blew Val over. Peter said something she didn't hear.

"We'll see you Sunday, okay?" Val hung up the phone without waiting for a response, her gaze never leaving Layla and the strange boy she was with.

Val's pulse quickened as she spied on Layla from behind a wall of lacy lingerie. Christ, no wonder Layla didn't want to be seen with her; she was incredibly embarrassing. In fact, Val was mortified on Layla's behalf.

But she couldn't help it.

Here was her daughter, flirting, maybe. Blossoming into a woman right before her eyes. Really, though, Val could do without the sight. Since when was Layla interested in boys?

Wasn't it too soon?

It took a moment for Val to dig around in the archives of her brain for her first kiss. Was it fourteen? Why hadn't she considered this? Was Layla going to be an early bloomer like herself?

She wavered for a moment, frozen by indecision. If she stepped out from behind this lovely display of sexy undies, she would certainly traumatize Layla in front of a boy she liked. But if Val stayed put, what would happen? A mental image of Layla and this strange boy kissing right there at the checkout counter caused her breath to catch. No, that wasn't going to happen.

With renewed determination, Val juggled the articles of clothing she held in her hands and walked confidently in their direction. Instead of humiliating her daughter, she would just pay for these clothes as if she didn't know Layla at all. Yes, that was what she was going to do.

She strode to the counter, trying so hard to avoid eye contact with Layla, but failing miserably. At Layla's horrified face, Val offered a small smile and assessed the boy behind the counter. Tall and lanky, wearing clothes his mother probably laid out for him. Dillon, if his name tag was correct. Val hadn't heard of a Dillon. Was he from school? If he was working here at the department store, he had to be at least sixteen, and that thought sprung Val right out of her skin. There was no way she could pretend here any longer.

"Hi, honey," she said to Layla, hoping the tone of her voice conveyed the message that they would definitely be discussing this in the car. "Who's your friend?" Friend? Boyfriend? If this was her boyfriend, what was Val going to do? She was too young to have a boyfriend. She wasn't even on birth control yet. Val's thoughts began to spiral, and she tried to remember when she started taking the pill. Why couldn't she remember?

Layla caved in on herself, her shoulders hunched forward. "God, Mom!" She met Val's gaze, the scowl on her face deadly. "This is Dillon, he's a *friend*." Layla's eyes widened as she emphasized the word "friend."

Val leaned back a bit and held up a hand. Just friends, got it. A wave of relief washed over her.

"Dillon, this is my mom." Layla groaned the words as if just saying them out loud was embarrassment enough.

"Do you want me to ring those up for you, ma'am?" Dillon's voice was a little shaky, like he didn't know if calling her ma'am was the right thing to do. As if he didn't know what sort of reaction she might have to that. He held out his arms to take the items from her, his bones protruding from every joint. Did the boy even know how to eat?

Val peeked down at the clothes clutched to her chest. A cream-colored bralette with a bow in the middle, a black racer-back sports bra, and a package of plain jane cotton undies. Beside her, Layla covered her eyes and groaned.

Was this a make-it-or-break-it moment? One that would set Layla up for years of therapy if she didn't make the right choice?

Clutching the clothes protectively, Val backed up and said, "You know what? I think I have some more shopping to do." She glanced quickly at her watch and then at Layla. "Thirty minutes," she said as she scurried out of there.

· · · ·

VAL WAITED UNTIL SHE had the car on the highway before confronting Layla. She needed to be going at least forty-five mph to ensure that Layla wouldn't just open the door and fling herself out of the car to avoid the conversation. Not that Val thought she would, but teenagers didn't always make the best choices, so it was better to be safe.

"So tell me about Dillon," she said in an *I'm not your mother, I'm your friend!* kind of tone.

Layla slouched in her seat and stared out the window. Silence.

"Are you two..." Val didn't want to say the words. She didn't want to ask if this was Layla's first boyfriend but didn't know how else to phrase it.

"I told you! He's my friend."

"Just making sure, honey." Her grip tightened on the steering wheel. "You know, sometimes friends can become more than friends quicker than you might think. I just want you to be—"

"Stop, please, I don't want to talk about this!" And to double down on those words, Layla pulled her phone out of her bag and shoved earbuds into her ears.

Val sighed, cursed the afternoon sun, and tried not to think about the next three years living with this beast of a child. She had to get through to Layla, but Val hadn't the slightest idea how.

Chapter 5

Evelyn, her court-ordered therapist, reminded Val of Librarian Barbie. Tall, blond, conventionally attractive, and could probably get her rocks off by charging late fees. She wore a crisp, white blouse tucked into a hip-hugging, black pencil skirt and towered over Val in ruby red heels that accentuated her already eye-popping calf muscles. A cyclist, perhaps? Trail runner? Mountain climber? Was Val the only one in town who didn't actively enjoy nature?

Val hadn't been expecting Eveyln's office to be so pristine with bright white walls and bougie gold accents. The furniture, also white, which felt like a bold choice, even held a brand new smell. She was suddenly very aware of her ratty cutoffs and gnarly toenails on full display in her flip-flops. When was the last time she cut those suckers? Sadly, her mother's love for properly trimmed and painted nails didn't rub off on her. In fact, her mom would be incredibly disappointed if she got a glimpse of Val's feet right now. Val tucked them under the chair and tried not to care. It figured, she was only five minutes into her therapy session, and her mother had to weasel her way into her brain.

Evelyn sat across from her, back as straight as a pin, her eyebrows raised like she awaited Val's response to something. Val shook her mother out of her head and shifted in her chair.

"Uh, sorry, can you repeat the question?" Val said.

"Tell me what happened that day." Evelyn's voice was calm and inviting, like she'd been doing this for a while, fully expecting her demeanor to persuade Val to immediately spill her guts.

Val quirked a smile. She wasn't about to fall for it. "I think you already know."

"I have a police report, yes. But I prefer to have the events in your own words if you don't mind." Eveyln's face was the picture of neutral.

Telling this stranger everything was not appealing, but neither was paying for these sessions. If Val didn't want to drag these out, she would have to come up with something.

She shrugged and went for the truth. "I let my feelings get the better of me, I guess. I don't normally go around punching people, believe it or not."

Evelyn had a notebook on her lap and a pen poised, ready to take notes. "What feelings got the better of you?"

Please. Like she didn't know. Would it even matter what she said? Was Evelyn going to write it down and talk to the judge? What if Val said, *Disgust. His face was just so punchable*? Would that have some profound effect on these sessions? She briefly entertained the thought of testing that one out just to see where it landed, but dollar signs flashed in her mind, and she again went for truth. If for no other reason than to be done with this as quickly as possible.

"I was pissed off."

Evelyn didn't respond right away, just continued to focus her attention on Val, waiting for her to elaborate.

Val crossed her arms over her chest and stared back. She'd answered the question, what more needed to be said?

Clearly realizing that Val wasn't going to budge, Evelyn finally asked, "What pissed you off?"

What didn't? Dog turds on the sidewalk, the warming planet, a daughter who barely talks to her, the patriarchy? Take your pick.

"Well, I was fired from my job, for one."

Evelyn made a note. "Okay. Two?" Val held in a groan. They'd be here all day at this rate.

"I was fighting with my ex." Her hands flew up as she talked as if to say, "that's it, you got me."

Again, Evelyn waited a few beats before continuing. "What were you fighting about?"

"I don't even remember." Val's leg jiggled under the chair.

Glancing down at the papers in her lap, Evelyn said in a soft tone, one you would use with a child, "You told the judge that your mother has dementia. And you're the sole caretaker."

Okay, she wasn't exactly the sole caretaker. Coming to hold her mom's hand or change her sheets a few times a week hardly counted as caretaking. But it also hadn't exactly been a lie. She had been hoping to earn some sympathy points with the judge, and given the fact that she was here in this office instead of wearing an orange vest and picking up trash along the side of the road, maybe she had.

Val swallowed hard. She didn't really want to talk about her mom right now. So she raised one shoulder like it was no big deal.

"That sounds like a lot to deal with." Evelyn's face exuded compassion, and it took Val a moment to realize what was going on here. To see the dots that Evelyn incorrectly connected.

Val shook her head. "Oh, no. No. Taking care of my mom had nothing to do with why I'm here." Because if it did, she would have to talk about it. And that was not happening.

Evelyn just blinked as if waiting for Val to say more. Val stared back.

Finally, Evelyn shifted in her seat and said, "Okay. What did your daughter think of you punching a stranger?"

What a question. There was a time Layla might have been impressed by her actions, giving a dirtbag a run for his money, but Val couldn't tell what her reaction had been. She was annoyed. Always annoyed.

"Well, she doesn't think I'm hot shit, that's for sure."

"Do you think you're hot shit?"

Val sat there, stunned. Is this how these sessions were going to go? Val had never hated opening her mouth more in her life. How was she going to get through eight of these?

Evelyn sat forward in her chair, a tight-lipped smile on her face. "How about we do something a little different?"

Great, can't wait. Val threw her hands up. "Sure, why not?" Anything would be better than this.

"You're a writer, correct?"

Was she? Could she call herself a writer if no one was paying her to write?

"Yup."

"All right. Then I have an assignment for you."

• • • •

"SHE'S MAKING ME WRITE letters! Can you believe that? Like I'm some child sending an aunt I've never met a thank-you note for a shitty birthday gift," Val said, wiping the condensation off the sangria glass.

Her oldest friend, Rupa, sat next to her at the bar, a sly smile on her face.

"How horrible," she said with a laugh. Her ultra-white teeth practically glowed against her mahogany skin.

"Hey, it *is* horrible! Not only do I have to endure an hour of awkward conversation every week, but now I have homework on top of it."

Rupa pounded the table and said, "You're right! What a bitch!"

Grateful for the support, regardless of how fake it was, Val bumped Rupa's shoulder with hers. "Thank you."

After that brain-numbing adventure with Evelyn, Val had walked into The Whale ready for a drink with what Layla's generation would call her bestie. The bar, a popular late-night hangout for college students, was hopping with the happy hour crowd, i.e. people too lazy to leave the house after seven p.m.

"What kind of letters?" Rupa topped off their glasses from the pitcher of sangria. "Like letters to your old self?"

Now that would be the end of Evelyn right there. Val would rather go back to court and plead her case in front of a jury than be assigned letters to her old self. She couldn't stand something so cliché.

"She wants me to get in touch with my feelings, I guess. And because I have difficulty articulating them with my mouth, she thought pen and paper might be easier." Evelyn might have had a point with that one, but Val would never admit it out loud.

Rupa rested her chin on her palm. "That's not a bad idea. Who are you going to write letters to?"

Val shrugged. "She's leaving that up to me. She just wants me to get my feelings out. I don't know if I'm going to do it. It's so stupid."

A server dropped a basket of fresh tortilla chips onto their table, and Val dug in, loading up a chip with fresh guacamole and cramming the entire thing straight into her mouth.

"It's not stupid. Writing it down might be really helpful." Rupa shrugged. "At least try it. Maybe start with a letter to Peter."

The laugh that burst out of Val threatened to send food particles all over the bar. Val brought her napkin up to her face, covering her mouth as she chewed.

"A letter to Peter?" she said once everything was sufficiently masticated and down her throat. "Easy, I can do that one right now." She rifled through her purse and pulled out a grocery receipt and a pen. She scribbled really quick, folded the paper up, and shoved it back into her purse. "There. Done."

Rupa raised an eyebrow. "What does it say?"

"None of your business! But you're right, I do feel better."

"See, I knew—"

Val raised a hand to cut her off. "Can we not talk about this anymore, please? I already have one therapist, I don't need another."

"Okay, okay. This is your very belated birthday celebration, after all." Rupa held up her glass of sangria in a toast. "I'm so sorry I wasn't here for it, but happy birthday!"

Val clinked her glass. "Hey, you finally got to tour with the band, so I won't hold this one against you."

"Yes, and it was amazing, but damn, I'm so happy to be home. My plants missed me." She giggled. "And now we can celebrate your birthday!"

"You know I didn't want to do anything for my birthday." The constant crack of her kneecap whenever she took the stairs was the only reminder of aging that she needed. And she certainly didn't need that.

Rupa swatted at the air. "Please, we need to celebrate getting older and wiser." She placed her hand over the side of her mouth and leaned in conspiratorially. "This is the decade where our sex drives are going to peak! Bow chica wow wow!" Her shoulders shimmied, and she waggled her eyebrows. "And you, Miss Divorced, can go out and get it anytime you want!"

Val barked out a laugh. "Yes, I scream sex goddess right now."

Rupa's gaze drifted down from her Smashing Pumpkins T-shirt and faded jeans to the scuffed Vans on Val's feet. She frowned. "No. Not dating anyone, I take it?"

Of course, Val had entertained the idea from time to time, for no other reason than to have an orgasm that she didn't have to initiate. But it all felt exhausting.

"I don't have many selling points." Val put her hands on her hips, smiled a fake, beauty pageant-type of smile, and in a valley girl voice said, "Hi, I'm an unemployed writer with a teenage daughter who despises me, and the court thinks I have anger issues. I'm the whole package!" She set her glass down and dramatically tossed her hair like she was in a shampoo commercial. Instead of bouncing around seductively, her thin brown locks hung there like limp noodles.

Rupa shook her head, tucking a lock of sleek black hair behind her ear. "I honestly can't believe you punched a guy in the nose. You might be an asshole, but I would never peg you for the violent type."

"Just a bad day."

Rupa placed a hand on Val's shoulder, her eyes full of concern, like Val was suddenly a fragile doll. "Is everything okay with your mom? I mean, I know it's not okay, just...did something happen?" She said these words tentatively, and why wouldn't she? Rupa knew the situation with her mother and was fully aware of how Val despised talking about her.

Val waved her hand in the air, dismissing the question, and poured the rest of the fruity drink down her throat. "She's the same. It was just a really shitty day, that's all."

Rupa looked at the table. "I'm sorry." She placed her hand over Val's. The pads of her fingers were rough with calluses from decades of playing the guitar. "I'm glad you're finally in therapy. Oh, don't give me that look, you've been screwed up since the day I met you. I'm just happy someone else gets to listen to your shit."

Val socked her in the arm, and Rupa came in for another hug.

"Enough of this touchy-feely stuff, I know how much you hate it. Look, I know that turning forty is hard for some, but I'm going to embrace it and take advantage of the fact that I'm much more mature now than I was even ten years ago."

"Oh, yeah? And how are you going to do that?"

Rupa leaned forward and placed her elbows on the table. "I'm going to pick up a self-improvement challenge. You know, focus on one thing for the entire year and come out a better person in the end."

Val shot her a dubious look. "Like what?"

"Well, there's so much for you to choose from. Running a marathon. Starting a gratitude journal."

Val scoffed at those ideas. "Nothing with exercise, thanks." A gratitude journal? Not a chance in hell.

"I'm going to hike every day for a year," Rupa said, smiling.

"Why?" Val's thighs ached just thinking about it.

"Hiking brings me so much joy, but I don't do it enough. Plus, my new place is right near a cute little trail, so I really have no excuse." She picked a chip from the basket and scooped up some pico de gallo.

"By the end of the year, I'll have a clearer head and stronger muscles. Self-improvement! You should think about it." She crunched the chip, looking smug and satisfied.

"Would you two like a refill?" The bartender, a tall woman with long blond hair piled high on her head, smiled in their direction, reaching toward the empty pitcher.

"Yes, please! Thank you, Gina!" Rupa said with a flirty smile. She turned back to Val and said, "Gina's great. She's always looking out for me when I perform here."

The racer-back tank Gina wore showed off her tanned shoulders, her back muscles rippling as she pulled down a tumbler from the shelf above her. An expert at multitasking, her movements were quick and precise, like she had juggled glassware in preparation for this job. Gina placed a drink on the bar in front of another patron, picked up the now full pitcher, and returned it to their table.

"Enjoy," she said in a light and airy tone, close enough to Val's ear that her chest vibrated, as if a chord had been strummed somewhere deep within. Gina winked, a lopsided grin on her face, and Val's mouth pulled up into a matching smile that she absolutely couldn't help.

"Jesus," Rupa muttered, pouring them each another glass. "I bet the people across the room could feel those sparks." She gave Val a knowing look.

"Please." Val rolled her eyes, even though sparks had definitely been felt on her end. Something that hadn't happened in, well, she couldn't remember the last time.

"What's it like being attracted to everyone? I'm not sure my libido could handle the overload."

Val barked out a laugh. "I might live on the 'hearts not parts' bandwagon, but I'm just not attracted to that many people. I mean, are you attracted to every guy you see?"

Rupa gazed about the room, a dreamy expression on her face. "Yeah, kind of."

"Okay, you're a bad example." Val shook her head and took a sip of her drink. "I can count on one hand the number of people I've been attracted to in the last five years."

Rupa furrowed her brows. "Peter being one of them?"

"The thought of Peter makes my uterus turn to stone," Val deadpanned.

Rupa arched an eyebrow, a mischievous expression on her face. "I know for a fact that's not always been the case. You guys were good once. Well, twice, I guess. High school sweethearts that part ways and find each other again after college? That's pretty amazing when you think about it. I forget, why did you break up in the first place? Was he just as arrogant back then as he is now?"

But Val had stopped listening. Even though decades had passed, thoughts of that time in her life still brought up complicated feelings. And she didn't want to feel any of them right now.

"Can we not talk about Peter, please?" Val's voice came out more gruff than she would have liked, but Rupa didn't seem to notice.

Rupa put both her hands under her chin, her face bright and mischievous. "Well, how about I tell you all about this guy I met this summer? He—"

"No, I don't want to hear about your love life, either. Can we just move on?"

After a long-suffering sigh, Rupa said, "Fine. We can move on to more boring topics. Like work. What are you doing now that you're not at the magazine?"

"Oh, I'll be back at the magazine before you know it." It was the only thing she could think to do if she wanted to avoid a job at Whole Foods. She shuddered at the thought. Having to smile at people while selling them overpriced, albeit delicious, cheese? The horror.

Rupa looked dubious. "But you were fired. How do you plan on getting it back?"

"I'm going to write an article Sonia won't be able to turn down. Something big and amazing that she won't have any other choice than to give me my column back."

If only Val knew what that was.

Chapter 6

Val jiggled the keys in the lock. Damn it, the door was jammed. When was she going to have someone fix that? She threw her shoulder into the door at the same time that she pulled up on the handle, making sure her key was inserted in "just so." The door finally gave way, and she stumbled into the house. Her foot caught on the leg of the entry table, sending her sprawling to the floor, the mail sliding out of her hands and across the tile.

"Damn it!" Thank god Layla was at Peter's this weekend; she could swear freely without judgment. Sitting up as gingerly as she could, she rubbed her ankle. The last thing she needed was a trip to the ER. She made slow circles with her foot. It was fine.

"Asshole," she yelled to no one.

She put "fix the door" on her mental to-do list. Then again, if she had such trouble getting into the house, it also meant that a burglar or a rapist or a home invasionist (was that what they called themselves?) would struggle so much they would probably give up trying. Maybe she should just leave it.

Val stood, kicked off her sandals, and abandoned her purse on the floor to pick up the mail. She rifled through the junk, tossing them one by one into the recycling until she came across an envelope from Foothills Village. An overdue notice, no doubt. Her gut twisted at the thought of having to move her mom into a less expensive but even more depressing facility. She might not deserve the best of the best, but Val didn't want to see her neglected, sitting in her own filth. That would remind her too much of childhood. Though Val had never been left sitting in literal filth, just alone with the metaphorical kind.

She shoved her feelings down and tossed the envelope onto the stack of unpaid bills piled up on her counter. At some point, she'd get to them. But now was not that time. She moved to the air vent on the wall and spread her arms wide, letting the cool air dry her pits. Oh, sweet air conditioning! The oppressive heat from July had charged its way into August, with highs in the nineties most days. Between her overactive sweat glands and a sun that could fry her skin on contact, she had little desire to leave her house.

Maybe she should hightail it somewhere snowy and cold. Canada? Live out the rest of her days cuddled in a big, bulky sweater under a fleece blanket and in front of a fire. Heaven. She laughed at herself, acting like she was on the verge of death. Forty wasn't so terrible, right? Older, wiser, but not dead yet. Although, she wasn't sure about that wiser part. She was clearly still making decisions a twenty-something would make. Maybe Rupa was right. She could do with a little self-improvement. What could it hurt?

Finally getting enough of the sweet cold air, her nipples straighter than she'd ever be, she shook out her arms and picked her stuff up off the floor. She hung her keys on the hook by the door and pulled her phone out of her purse. The piece of paper she had folded up earlier floated to the ground. Right, the letter.

She unfolded it and read the words she scrawled to Peter.

Eat shit.

Val barked out a laugh. Sangria was still singing in her veins, and even though she was tired, she felt so freaking good. She ran a finger over the letter in her hand. Those two words were so simple, so to the point, and even though she had said them out loud more times than she could count, writing them made them take on a whole new meaning. It was satisfying. If only she could tell everyone who had ever pissed her off to just go screw themselves.

But then again, why couldn't she?

And that was when it hit her. That was going to be her forty-year challenge. Forty letters. Write one letter for every year of her life. Easy! She was a writer, after all.

Gleeful laughter bubbled up out of her as she removed her phone and opened her notes app. She would write a letter to…well, anyone who ticked her off. Better to write it than say it. She'd stay out of trouble this way. And she could appease Evelyn at the same time. Her fingers flew over the screen.

To the asshole who cut me off this morning:

Does driving 60 mph down Arapahoe Ave. make you feel like a big, strong man? Do you need to drive an impossibly expensive car to feel good about yourself? Are you compensating here? You are not special! And your car sucks.

Dear Joshua Sunders,

When you decided to snap my bra strap in fourth grade, did you realize that was the first day I ever wore one? Did you know that made me self-conscious for years to come? You're lucky I didn't bust your nose because apparently that's something I do now.

Val cackled to herself. This was incredibly juvenile but brought her so much joy, she couldn't stop. She typed out a letter to the phone company for all the absurd fees they charge, to Cokehead Cari for stealing her job, to the jerk who broke into her car in high school, and the guy who stole a package off her porch last month (joke was on him, though, it was a bulk order of tampons).

By the end of her rant, she had checked off ten of those letters already. Well, they were more like little missives rather than letters, but she was going to count them. And sure, they weren't her best work. But she never could write after a few drinks. It was good enough, however, to satisfy that little part of her brain that was compelled to complete a task. It was now acceptable for her to pass out.

Chapter 7

Val flung her bag into the back corner booth of her favorite local diner, The Greasy Spoon. It was her favorite because the name alone implied a fatty meal, something most of the people here weren't a fan of. Boulder was full of marathon runners and cyclists, cramming as much protein in their gullets as they could manage. But indulging in fat? Never! Val, however, loved her scrambled eggs fried up in a pan of rich, sizzling butter, a plate of crispy bacon on the side. Fat meant taste, didn't they know that?

"What can I get you?" Barb smiled down at her, a pencil lodged behind her ear, an order book in her hand. Her thin copper hair was pulled back in a bun, little wisps framing her saggy face. Barb was in her late sixties and was like one of those sweet and sour candies. At first, pleasing and delicious, and then all of a sudden, *BAM!* a tart punch to the face. Val never knew which side she might get on any given day, and that was thrilling. She might even consider Barb a hero of sorts.

"Hi, Barb," Val tossed her a big toothy smile, "just a coffee for me, please." She added a bat of her eyelashes for good measure.

Barb, to her credit, didn't bother with an eyeroll or an exasperated sigh. She just shot daggers at Val with her eyes, her sour side on full display.

"Your friend better order some food, that's all I'm saying."

Val kept her smile in place and said, "Well, she's the one with the job right now, so I would think so."

Val had been meeting up with Maddie every Tuesday morning during her unemployment. Maddie would share any gossip and intel from the office, the two of them scheming how to get Val back up there as part of the staff. Well, Val was scheming. Maddie probably thought this was just a weekly breakfast between friends.

She sent a silent plea to Maddie to get here soon with an empty stomach. It wasn't clear how long Barb would put up with her hogging a booth with only a coffee order. But it was all she could afford right now.

"Thanks, Barb!" she hollered as Barb walked away, her voice all syrupy sweet.

Val checked her phone, 8:45 a.m. Fifteen minutes was enough time to get some work done, so she pulled out her laptop while she waited. The previous night had been spent brainstorming a list of people she could write to. People who had wronged her, pissed her off, or were just general garbage humans. She couldn't remember the last time she was filled with so much glee. There must be something to this whole self-improvement bit; her mood had improved drastically. If only it could manifest an upgrade to her finances.

Opening a new document, she filtered through the list of people in her head. Which one of those pinheads was going to get told off today? Not that they really would, she would never send these, but there was just something so therapeutic about writing it all down.

Ping. A new email notification flashed on her screen. Sonia. Val narrowed her eyes in preparation. This obviously wasn't any good news. Another article rejection for sure. And why not, Sonia had rejected every single one Val had submitted so far. It definitely wasn't going to say, *We deeply regret our decision to let you go. Please accept this gigantic bonus of one million dollars along with your weekly column back. We kicked Cari to the curb.* No, that would never happen.

That kind of news would show up in the form of a phone call, or if Sonia ever had a desperate moment, maybe a grand gesture of sorts. An image popped into her head of Sonia, decked out in her usual hiking gear, holding up a boombox, Lloyd Dobler-style, outside of her bedroom window. Sadly, it was just as likely that Sonia would have her assistant send Val a fruit basket as an apology, which was not likely at all. If her former boss was sending an email, it was something she didn't want to hear.

Right now, she was jazzed and didn't want to ruin her good mood. So before bothering to read said email, Val focused on her new document and let her feelings loose.

Dear Soul-Sucking Bottom Feeders of Mile High Magazine,

She had Cari in mind as she typed, but really everyone there, Maddie excluded, were useless turds.

I have hated every minute of writing for your stupid magazine.

She had loved it. When she was offered the position, she had been an out-of-her-mind stay-at-home mom, tweeting sarcastic lines about the frequency of baby poop. Everyone thought she was hilarious, but she was drowning in the tedium of it all. The full-time writing gig saved her life.

No one reads your contrived shit. I hope Cari writes something racist or homophobic, and it brings you giant buttholes down.

Now this was plausible. Inevitable, maybe. The staff was overwhelmingly white; it was only a matter of time before someone made a grave error.

She twittered in delight as she typed, her shoulder dancing a little shimmy. It had been a while since writing had brought her such joy. Well, what better way to ruin a good mood than to read an email from Sonia? She sighed as she clicked it open, steeling herself for another rejection.

"Ugh!" Val pounded a fist on the table. She had been expecting this exact thing, but it was still hard to take. If Sonia would just accept one of her articles, she would be that much closer to getting her column back. Didn't Sonia know that she was a fountain of ideas? Val kept a spark sheet of thoughts and storylines in her notes app. And it was loaded with a crap-ton of project potential. She just needed to find the right one with the perfect angle. But what?

"Sorry, I'm late!" Maddie plopped down onto the bench opposite her.

Val didn't even bother looking up from her screen.

"Mad, it's fine, it's just after nine. No one else would consider that late. Listen, I just got an email from Sonia. She's not printing my article, but whatever, I took a lot of it from something I wrote a few years ago. Because, come on, neighborhoods are going to keep bouncing back from a wildfire. They just do. It feels like that's all we write about sometimes. Anyway, so I was thinking—"

"Val!" Her name shouted at such a high volume that customers turned in their seats to see what the fuss was about finally pulled Val's gaze away from her laptop. Maddie sat with her shoulders more slumped than usual, curling her up like a pillbug. Dark half moons puffed under her eyes as tears streaked through a half-assed attempt at concealer.

"Oh, Maddie." Val reached a hand across the table and touched Maddie's arm. "What's wrong?"

"Meredith left!" Those two simple words ripped out of Maddie with a gut-wrenching sob. While Val often found Maddie's displays of emotions to be dramatic and irritating, this one tore right through her chest, too.

Val got up and squished herself next to Maddie, her arm rubbing circles on Maddie's back. This form of physical contact with someone Val had only had a professional relationship with was weird and out of her comfort zone. But right now, Maddie reminded Val of Layla, drowning in an overwhelming sea of emotions. She let her motherly instincts kick in.

"Hey, shh, it's going to be okay." Obviously, Val didn't have a clue, but that was what someone nice and caring would say, right? "What happened?"

Maddie blew her nose into a napkin. "I don't know. They just packed their stuff and left."

Val squinched up her face. Meredith and Maddie had been partners for a few years; there had to be more to the story. But she didn't say anything, just kept up the circles.

Maddie took in a huge breath and let it out slow.

"Well, we had a fight. I mean, sort of. They just...they haven't been happy for a while, and I just don't know how to make them happy, I guess." Another round of sobs eked out of her.

"Yeah, relationships are tough," Val said in her most motherly voice. "Breakups are even harder." Truer words hadn't come out of her mouth in what felt like weeks, months even. Her breakup with Peter had been brutal. It had been years in the making, and she had seen it coming, but it didn't make it any easier.

"Do you want to order some pancakes?" Val offered. "I make pancakes for Layla when she's having a tough time." Which was always, it seemed.

Maddie shook her head. "No, Sonia moved up our meeting and..." She checked her phone and promptly shoved it into her bag, throwing the strap over her shoulder. "Shoot, I have to leave. I'm sorry."

Val got up and let Maddie out of the booth. "I'll see you next week, okay?"

There should have been some comforting words Val could send Maddie off with, but right now, they weren't coming. Maddie and Val were just two people who shared a cubicle wall once upon a time. Comforting her through an emotional breakdown didn't make them friends, did it? She heaved a sigh and sat down right as her own phone pinged with a new text.

Layla. Val would never tell Peter this, but getting Layla a new phone with a tracking feature had been a dream come true. An upgrade to a smartphone had been a bit nerve wracking for Val, but Peter, the tech whiz that he was, secured all the parental controls and made sure she couldn't do anything too stupid on it.

Layla: *I'm going to Daisy's after school.*

This was not an ask but more like a heads up. Was that how it worked now? Did Layla call the shots? What were parents even for these days?

Val: *Okay, but I'm making tacos for dinner, so be home by 6:30.*
Layla: *They're ordering sushi, we can have tacos tomorrow.*
Of course they're ordering sushi.
Val: *Fine, but be home by 8 p.m., it's a school night.*
Layla: *Fine*
Val: *heart emoji*
"So."

Val nearly jumped out of her seat at the sound of Barb's voice. She was standing next to the booth, a hand on one hip and a coffee cup in the other. Val let out a shaky breath and clutched her chest.

"Christ, Barb, you scared me!" Val could actually picture her in a horror movie—the crotchety server who slaughtered customers with steak knives if they didn't order the right amount of food.

Barb placed a mug of coffee on the table. "I see your friend left." Her eyes narrowed. "I take it this is all you're ordering. Again?"

Val glanced at the door and wondered if she should lie and tell Barb that Maddie would be right back. But there were other customers in the diner, so surely Barb wouldn't try slitting her throat, would she?

Sighing, Val said, "She had to step out for a minute." Her phone pinged again, and Val glanced down.

Layla: *eyeroll emoji*

"Hot date, tonight?" Barb eyed the phone in Val's hand.

Ha! A hot date? What even was that? Had Val ever had a hot date in her life? She flashed Barb a smile. "No, just texting my daughter. She's a teenager, so you know, she doesn't want to have dinner with me."

Barb grunted. "I remember the teenage years. It's funny, your kids really come into their own and then you, as a parent...man, it's really a make-it-or-break-it time." She shook her head.

Val frowned. "What do you mean?"

Barb leaned on the side of the booth, her voice low. "It's super easy to screw 'em up at that age, that's all I'm saying." She stood back up and paused a moment before she added, "My daughter doesn't speak to me anymore." Her shoulders slumped as she walked away.

Val scoffed. Layla might be prickly at times, but there was no way they would end up like that.

"Oh," Barb said over her shoulder, "next time, you're ordering food, or you sit at the counter. That booth is for food service." She pointed a finger at Val from across the room.

Val lifted her hand in salute. "Yes, ma'am."

Chapter 8

Val jiggled her leg as she waited for her second therapy session, her arms over her chest, wondering if this one could possibly be any worse than the last. Evelyn sat across from her in her bright white armchair. Her thighs were again hugged into a black pencil skirt, her legs crossed at the ankles with forest green pumps on her feet this time. Val had remembered to class it up, but for her, that meant wearing a pair of jeans and hiding her feet.

Evelyn had that look again. The open, friendly one where her mouth wasn't actually smiling, but the rest of her muscles appeared to be. Or was that just Botox? Val imagined other patients spewing their deepest, darkest secrets to a face like that. Sharing their long desired kink that their partner refused to play out with them. Or revealing that they have a telescope in their bedroom that they use to spy on their curtainless neighbors. Val didn't have anything weird or scandalous to share. Sure, she punched a guy, and she was here to atone, that was it.

"You seem agitated," Evelyn said, her expression thoughtful.

Val scoffed. "Insightful."

"Does the silence make you uncomfortable?" Was it uncomfortable to have a stranger stare at her, expecting her to dive to the depths of her soul and open up about her mommy issues (which she certainly didn't have, thank you very much)?

Val just stared back at her and willed her leg to stop jostling. Evelyn cocked her head, her eyebrows raising ever so slightly, but Val stayed mute.

"How about we start with you telling me what's new since the last time you were here?" Evelyn's gaze drifted down to the notebook in her lap as if she were checking up on what she wrote down during their last session. Val had barely shared anything; what could she have written?

"Well, my bank account is now hundreds of dollars lighter." Val let out an unamused laugh, but Evelyn's face was impassive.

"How did your assignment go?" Evelyn's pen was now poised over her paper, ready to write *total failure* all over the page, certainly.

Val sat a little straighter in her seat. "I did write a letter, and I can't believe I'm going to say this, but it actually felt great." Which was true. Sure, she didn't exactly follow Evelyn's parameters, but Val wasn't one for rules.

Instead of saying anything, Evelyn gave an encouraging look, like she wanted to hear more, and feeling a bit generous, Val added, "I wrote down how I had been feeling, and I felt so much better. Like a weight had been lifted."

Evelyn's eyes narrowed; she wasn't falling for any of this. "Really?" She sat back in her seat and leaned an elbow on the armrest.

"Yes! In fact, I'm expanding on your idea." It wouldn't hurt to toss Evelyn a compliment, would it?

She cocked an eyebrow, finally intrigued. "Please, tell me more."

"Well, turning forty wasn't something I was looking forward to, and my friend suggested commemorating it somehow. I'm going to do that by writing letters. You know, self-improvement stuff." Val met Evelyn's gaze, feeling quite proud of herself.

One would think that Evelyn was a mannequin if it weren't for the fact that she blinked from time to time. Val hadn't been expecting her to cheer and hand her some graduation certificate, but a little enthusiasm would be nice. She was over here taking initiative, wasn't she?

"I'm going to write forty letters before my next birthday," Val continued. "One for each year of my life. You know, to get stuff off my chest, so to speak."

This time, Evelyn nodded, but her lips pulled down in a slight frown. "I see. And what kind of stuff are you getting off your chest?"

Val shifted in her seat. "Well, like what you suggested. Instead of letting my feelings build up inside, I should let them out. You know, I can release my anger on the paper instead of on someone's face." She was hoping that would make Evelyn smile, but no dice.

Evelyn bent forward in her chair, leaning her elbows on her knees, her gaze locked on Val. "Do you think a plan of telling forty different people to fuck off is really going to help you?"

Damn! Why did she have to be so perceptive? Val threw her arms in the air and sank back into her chair. "Couldn't hurt, could it?"

"Yes, I think it could." Evelyn took a breath and focused a look on Val. "Getting your anger out on paper does have its benefits, sure. You might feel satisfied, vindicated even. However, dwelling on the negative could make it fester. And I have a suspicion that's how you ended up here, is it not?" She paused and gave Val a meaningful look.

Val held up her hands. "Let me stop you right there. If you're going to ask me to write something lovey dovey, just don't. That's not me."

"Anger isn't your only option, that's all I'm saying." Evelyn paused, but Val didn't know what to say. She was a tornado of emotions from time to time, and it was hard to pin them all down. Anger just happened to be the most accessible one of the bunch. Easy to grasp and channel.

"This week, I want you to write a letter of gratitude. Focusing a bit more on the positive might be a better route for releasing some of your anger. Don't get me wrong, I do believe a good *screw you* is necessary at times, but I don't want you getting bogged down by that and having it be your go-to response. It might be time to dig into your compassionate self."

Val couldn't believe what she was hearing. Write letters of compassion? Gratitude? Was she even capable of such emotions? She could only imagine that Evelyn would next ask her to write letters apologizing for stuff.

Invoking her inner teen, she slumped back in her chair, raised her face to the ceiling, and groaned. A full-on Layla groan. A *don't you ever knock?* kind of groan. What could she say, her bones may be forty years old, but her attitude was still developing.

Evelyn held up her hands, but she smiled. "Just try it. That's all I'm asking. Go home, pick one person in your life that you appreciate, and tell them why. Start with someone easy. A friend, maybe? Or your mother."

Her mother? Val bolted upright. "My mother doesn't deserve my gratitude. What would I even thank her for? She—" Val caught herself before she could finish that thought. She had said too much already. Evelyn had dangled a seemingly innocent little carrot, and Val had snapped it up without thinking.

Evelyn leaned forward in her chair, lapping it all up like childhood trauma was what she lived for.

Val coughed into her hand. "Gratitude is not my thing."

A small smile spread on Evelyn's face as she sat back in her chair. "So I see." She jotted something down in her notebook, and Val cursed her big, fat mouth.

Evelyn set her pen down and pursed her lips thoughtfully. "I don't have to remind you that at the end of this, I will have to make a recommendation to the courts. I imagine you would like that recommendation to be positive, yes?"

Hold up, was Evelyn threatening her? Can one actually fail therapy?

"Yes, Evelyn, I would." Val's voice held a stony edge to it.

"Okay, then just try it. You don't have to write to your mother, it was just a suggestion. Maybe start with someone whom you feel affection toward. Someone uncomplicated."

Deep down, Val understood the point, that telling people how stupid they were felt great in the moment but never fully made the anger go away. But it didn't make this assignment any more desirable.

She heaved a sigh. "Fine. I'll try it. Just for you."

Evelyn shook her pretty little head. "No, do it for you." She shrugged and added, "And maybe for the court."

Val rolled her eyes, and it finally clicked. Therapists were like parents.

Chapter 9

"I cooked up your favorite for dinner tonight!" Val yelled to Layla, who had finally emerged from the cave she'd been hiding in since school let out. She tried to make her voice as peppy as she could.

"We haven't had a chance to sit and chat for a while, I just want to know how your first week of school has been. Ninth grade! How's it feel to be a high schooler now?" It was hard to believe that Layla was old enough for high school. It felt like yesterday that Val sent her off to middle school, worried about her getting her period for the first time.

Val finished setting the table and realized that she was talking to no one. "Layla! Dinnertime!"

Layla appeared in the hall again, an unimpressed look on her face.

"Tuna mac!" Val placed the casserole dish on the table with a flourish. In one of the foodiest places in the country, leave it to her child to love something so disgusting. There had been an entire year that Layla ate nothing else for dinner. Half their pantry was full of boxes of mac and cheese and cans of tuna.

Val motioned for Layla to sit down and dig in. Instead, Layla heaved a sigh that could be heard around the world and rolled her eyes as far back into her head as possible.

"Mo-om!" Val knew she was in trouble if Layla turned mom into a two-syllable word. "I'm vegan now, I don't eat tuna. Or cheese." She made a face like the food had been cooked in a toilet. "I might have eaten this when I was, I don't know, thirteen, but I don't like it anymore." Val resisted the urge to point out that she was thirteen only a few months ago.

Val just shrugged. "I'm sorry, honey, I didn't know that. Maybe we could keep a sticky note on the fridge, and you can update it when your taste buds change." Which had been every few months since she was two. Layla did not look amused.

"Okay, if you want something else for dinner, you're welcome to make it."

Layla slumped into a chair and scooped up some of the tuna mac, plopping it onto her plate. The squelch of the wet noodles against the plastic serving spoon made Val want to gag.

"It's fine, I'll eat this one last time, I guess." If Layla's words had eyes, they were rolling all over the place.

Val sucked in a breath and plastered on a smile. "So, honey, the first week of high school! How was it?"

Layla stuffed a mouthful of cheesy pasta into her face and shrugged. Val hadn't expected much from the conversation as Layla had shared diddly-squat with her the first few days. She was still disappointed.

How did one get a teenager to talk? She'd ask her mom for help on this one, but, oh, right, she hadn't been there to talk to her at all. Val could still remember her first day of freshman year. The elation she felt at getting picked to write for the school newspaper when freshmen rarely did anything more than grunt work. She got to write! It had been her dream. The only thing she had wanted to do was share that joy with her mother, but by then, her mom had stopped coming home from work and instead went out with the girls. She had spent so much time as a single parent, she needed to find herself, leaving Val to cook her own dinners, find her own entertainment, and put herself to bed. Val hoped it had been worth it, finding herself. Because, by the looks of things now, her mother was more lost than ever.

Val tried a new tactic. "Meet any new people? Make any new friends?" Val picked at her salad, not wanting a mouth full of food if an opportunity to say something came up.

"Yeah, Mom, we all frolicked around the playground holding hands." Layla shoveled more food into her mouth, her attention on the phone in front of her.

THE FAKER'S GUIDE TO SELF-IMPROVEMENT

The sarcasm that oozed out of her was impressive. Val had to tamp down the pride that rose in her chest at not having to worry about Layla holding her own against some mansplainy boys in her class. Layla would be just fine in that department.

"What about, what's his name? From the mall?" Val held her breath. She wasn't sure what she wanted to hear, but it had been important to ask. What if she hung out with Dillon on a regular basis? What if they sneaked around when Layla was at Peter's place? She needed to know.

Layla's fork stopped midair, and her gaze shifted to Val. "What about him?" Her eyes narrowed, full of suspicion, like Val was about to accuse him of a nefarious act.

Val took a sip of water and tried to shake off the murdery vibes Layla was tossing her way. "Nothing. Just wondering if you guys hang out or whatever you call it."

Layla dropped her fork, the clank of metal against ceramic making Val jump in her seat. She pushed herself up from the table with a huff.

"I'm not hungry," she said as she stomped out of the room.

Val sighed and rubbed her forehead. She was used to her sparring matches with Peter, but Layla was bringing in some serious karate chops herself, throwing Val off balance. Where was the sweet little girl who used to tell her mommy everything? The one who would come home from school excited to curl up next to Val on the sofa and laugh about the weird things she did with her friends? Her eyes would get all wide and adorable, and she would ramble on so much that Val couldn't wait for her to shut up. Val's chest squeezed.

Layla hadn't done any of that in years, why was she missing it so much now?

Val finished her dinner, making a mental note to never make that trash again. She cleared the table, did the dishes, and made her way down the hall to check on Layla. If she was upset, maybe she needed someone to talk to.

Covered in a variety of colorful stickers, Layla's bedroom door screamed teenager. From the moment one laid eyes on it, they knew that inside was something of a Bermuda Triangle. An abyss where dirty dishes went missing, laundry appeared to triple, and nothing could ever be found without a good half hour of crying first.

Peter would have never let her adhere something so permanent to any piece of furniture, so for that very reason, Val had allowed her do it, letting her be the cool mom for once.

Among the smattering of National Park souvenirs and emoji stickers were quite a few local brewery logos. They had frequented many of the breweries as a family, and their stickers were admittedly cool. Though, seeing it like this, it was a little strange to let your teenager plaster beer logos all over the place.

Val spotted the *Badass Bitch* sticker that she had given Layla last year, and then her attention landed on the one next to it. "That's new," Val whispered to herself as she ran her finger over the newest addition to the sticker door. On a black background, bright yellow letters read, *Fuck Off*. Language, Layla.

Where had she gotten that? Not that it mattered. If Layla wanted to swear, Val was all for it, as long as she used the words correctly and didn't aim any of those words at her mom.

Val tapped her knuckles on the door.

"What?" The sound of Layla's voice would make anyone run for the hills. A tone of voice that stopped all questions in their tracks. Well, for any normal person anyway. Val saw it more as a challenge.

Val kept her voice light and positive, pretending she couldn't detect the homicidal tone. "Want some tea?"

Rustling came from behind the door as if Layla were tossing clothes into a pile. Oh, what if she was cleaning? The thought made Val put her hand on her chest, pride bubbling up in her. Then she laughed at herself because Layla's room hadn't been properly cleaned in two solid years.

"No, thanks," Layla said, her voice muffled.

Val stumbled backward. A "no, thanks"? Val's spirits lifted, Layla had remembered to say thank you. Through a door and not very nicely, but she would take it.

"Okay, good night, sweetie! I love you!" She kissed her palm and laid it flat against the door.

Layla mumbled something, and even though Val was certain it was "bite me" or even "screw you," she would just pretend Layla had said "I love you" back. When was the last time Layla had said that to her? Val sighed and went into the kitchen to put the kettle on.

With her Sleepytime tea in hand, Val cozied up in an armchair, throwing a light blanket over her lap. The windows were open, letting in the early September night air. It was perfect. The days might still be hot and sweaty, but the evenings! The only way Val could accurately describe a September evening in the foothills was with a chef's kiss. Some things were just too perfect for words.

She opened her laptop and stared at a blank document. If she was going to try her hand at this letter of gratitude thing, she might as well do it now, if for no other reason than to get it over with. Val racked her brain for someone to write to. Evelyn had said to start easy and small. A letter to her mother would have been the exact opposite: excruciating and monumental.

Val sipped at her tea, breathing in the herby, apple scent. Someone easy, uncomplicated. Was it ever easy to tell someone how much they mean to you, though? All her relationships right now felt complicated, tenuous. And she didn't want to thank some rando on the street for simply not being an asshole. That left her with one option: Rupa.

The only thing complicated about their relationship these days was the fact that they operated on opposite schedules. Val considered herself to be an early bird, not by choice, of course, her circadian rhythm just deemed it so. Which made Rupa more of a vampire. Aside from the belated birthday happy hour, Val couldn't remember the last time they met up before the sun started to fall.

Dear Rupa,

Val's fingers hovered over the keyboard, ready to strike those letters, but she didn't know where to start. "Thank you for being a friend" felt a bit too *Golden Girls*. Too cheesy. But telling someone how much they mean to you, to really put that into words was like ripping your chest open and exposing your heart. Baring your soul. It would require vulnerability. She shuddered.

According to Evelyn, there was a lesson to be learned here, and if she didn't learn it, the courts would find out. She closed her eyes, took a deep breath, and conjured up the first time she met Rupa their freshman year of college.

Decked out in a pair of ultra-short cutoffs that showed off her thick brown thighs, Rupa had been belting out a cover of *Brown Eyed Girl* over the quad. The sun had been setting, casting an orange glow over the grass. She danced across the stage, obviously lost in the music, and Val had been struck by how carefree she was. When Rupa smiled out over the audience, a love of life beamed from her face, and Val imagined getting lost in her twilight-colored eyes. Summoning courage from who knows where, Val had approached her after the set and asked her out for a drink. Rupa answered by slinging an arm over Val's shoulder and saying, "I'm straight as an arrow. Where should we go?" They had been friends ever since.

I don't know if you're aware, but you basically rescued me from being a weird loner for our college career. What made you say yes to drinks, I'll never know. And why you've stuck it out with me and my stubborn ass this long is a complete mystery, but I don't know where I'd be without you.

Stuck in her goth phase? Or maybe she would have stayed in her room every Friday night to study like a loser. Without Rupa, she could have graduated with honors and no social life to speak of.

You brought a ray of sunshine to my very dull existence, and I couldn't imagine my life without you in it.

66

Her insides went all warm and gooey. It was uncomfortable. She didn't like it.

Thank you for pulling me out of my hovel and making me see the world around me. And thank you for always loving me, even when I'm an asshole.

Her chest squeezed, and tears pricked at her eyes. Had she ever really told someone what they meant to her? Layla, sure. She told Layla she loved her every day, but that was different. Layla was her daughter.

I love you very much and am so lucky to call you my friend.

She typed the last sentence as fast as she could, slammed the laptop shut, and tossed it on the sofa like it was cursed to bring out all the emotions she had stuffed down.

There was obviously so much more she could have said. Rupa had been there through the divorce, offering encouragement and even a place to crash when it got really rough. Through all the drama with her mom. And she had always been exceptionally wonderful with Layla, despite being childfree herself. Val was suddenly overwhelmed by all the ways Rupa had made an impact on her life. This letter was highly inadequate.

The hot sting behind her eyes moved ever so slightly, and a tear slipped down her cheek. She wiped it away and blinked back the others threatening to spill. Jesus, what was wrong with her? Crying because her friend was too awesome? What kind of garbage was that?

A dull ache spread over her temples, like her head was being squeezed. This was the downside to feeling all the feelings, wasn't it? The emotional hangover that people talk about? Imagine what it would be like if she truly cried. Like a full-on ugly cry. Her head might explode.

After shaking out her hands, she picked up her phone to distract herself and get her back into a better frame of mind. A quick doom scroll should do the trick. But after seeing too many posts of ridiculously cute animals, Val had to pop out of social media before her heart melted anymore.

She dropped the phone into her lap and leaned her head back against the chair, her gaze falling on the kitchen counter and the stack of bills in the corner. It had been months since she had been fired from *Mile High Magazine*, and unemployment would run out eventually. She had to figure out a way to make some money. If only she could get her column back.

Val logged back into her phone and pulled up Maddie's contact. She needed to know what was going on at the office. What happened in the latest staff meeting? What was Cari writing about? And more importantly, could Val do it better? Of course, she could! If only they had a chance to chat about the office before Maddie ran out of the diner the other day, crying.

Oh, right. Her breakup.

Would it be too insensitive to ask Maddie for the hot goss? Val would be an asshole if she asked this right now, she was sure of it. Instead, she should play it safe and ask how Maddie's doing. Right? Be a friend. Not that she was, really. The only thing Val knew about Maddie was that she had an annoying habit of humming as she typed, which was especially aggravating when Val was trying to concentrate on an important article. Oh, and her favorite yogurt brand (Chobani), which Val might have swiped from the staff fridge a time or two.

She fired off a quick text before she could change her mind.

Val: *Hey, Mad, how are you holding up?*

Val didn't care, though, did she? Hearing all about Maddie's breakup drama sounded just as desirable as shoving a sharp pencil deep into her eardrum. Maddie's response was almost immediate.

Maddie: *Not great. Are you free to talk? Drinks, maybe?*

Val thought of the margaritas she would order if she went out with Maddie. Somewhere in the distance, her bank account screamed. She couldn't go out tonight, not just because Layla was home and she was close to broke. If she was going to get her job back, she had to focus, and she couldn't do that with a tequila hangover.

Val: *Not tonight.*

Something unpleasant niggled at the back of her brain. A feeling she wasn't accustomed to. Holy shit, was this guilt? Her conscience, maybe? Her thumbs seemed to think so because they worked their way over the little keyboard all on their own.

Val: *I could do coffee on Friday.*

Maddie: *Yes! See you then!*

Val slumped back in her chair, the dull ache around her temples moving swiftly to a rhythmic pounding. She was going to have to hear about the breakup whether she liked it or not. Damn it! If this was self-improvement, she wasn't sure she liked it.

Chapter 10

Val was hunched over her laptop at the kitchen counter when the front door slammed. Layla kicked off her shoes and threw her backpack to the ground, almost growling as she did so.

"Hey, what's wrong?" Val stood and mentally prepared herself for the worst. Did Layla fight with a friend? Get scolded by a teacher in front of the entire class? Or walk around all day with period-stained shorts? She sucked in a breath; that last one would be hard to recover from.

Layla made a Chewbacca-like grumble as she stomped down the hall. While many parents would give this sort of attitude a wide berth, Val was not one of those parents. She grabbed the tea she had just poured for herself and followed.

Layla's bedroom door slammed in Val's face. The mug of tea jostled in her hands, but the scalding water stayed put.

A new sticker on Layla's door read, *What the actual fuck?* Val couldn't agree more.

She knocked on the door. "Layla, honey." But there was no answer. "I'm coming in." Val pushed the door open and was greeted with the debris of a teenage-sized tornado. How did she find anything in here? Oh, that's right, she didn't.

Piles of laundry draped over the bed, clothes hung off the side, some already escaped to the floor like they might slink away at any moment. Books and papers scattered over the polka dot duvet, which made a Layla-sized lump in the middle of the bed.

Val tiptoed over the clutter on the floor, doing her best to step only on the rug, but it was hard. She reached a hand out and gingerly pushed the mass of clutter on Layla's nightstand over an inch. Just enough room for her to set the teacup down.

"I brought you a cup of chamomile." Val plopped down on the bed, right on top of the hump of blankets, aiming for Layla's backside.

"God, Mom!" Her voice muffled by the blankets, she squirmed under Val.

"Oh, I didn't see you there. All I saw was dirty laundry and," Val rifled through the papers on the bed, "is this homework?" And then her gaze landed on a stack of fliers, advertising extracurricular activities. "Ooh, are you joining a club?"

"Get off!" Layla pushed, and Val slid off the bed, a pile of clothes cushioning her fall. "And stop going through my stuff!" She flipped the blanket off her head and lunged for the papers still in Val's hands.

Unable to take a hint, Val said, "So what are you thinking? Yearbook? Drama?" She didn't think Layla would go for something athletic, but just to be fair, she added in a slightly skeptical voice, "Track?"

"Mom!" Layla snatched the fliers from her hands. "I said stop!"

The adolescent force was strong with this one. "All right, fine," Val said, standing. She folded her arms across her chest. "What crawled up your butt today?"

"Ugh!" Layla groaned and tossed the covers back over her head. "Just leave me alone."

Val made a little space at the end of her bed and sat back down. "Seriously, though, jellybean, what's going on? Did something happen today?"

"Yes, Mom!" Layla used her best "You're the Dumbest Person on the Planet" voice. "Lots of things happened today. I went to school, I ate lunch, and now I'm home."

Val reached out and rubbed what she assumed were Layla's feet. "And why did you barrel into the house like the sky was raining dog turds?"

The blanket flew off Layla's face once more, and she stared up at her mother. Her soft brown curls fanned out over her pillow, tear stains on her cheeks. "A group of kids were being assholes to Dillon, and I tried to stop them. And now they're starting rumors about us."

THE FAKER'S GUIDE TO SELF-IMPROVEMENT

"Oh, honey." Val's chest squeezed.

This was the stuff she wasn't prepared for as a parent. She wasn't equipped to tell her child how to handle a bully. Punch them in the face? Break their nose? Obviously, Layla needed more advanced techniques. Val's were too old school and would most likely get her suspended.

"Kids suck. Give it time, they'll find someone else to pick on soon."

"It just made me feel so stupid." Layla hid under her blankets once more, and Val could hear her holding back a sob.

"I'm sorry that happened." She gave Layla's foot a squeeze through the blanket. "How about I make us some popcorn and we can watch a movie?" The piles of papers on Layla's bed crinkled as Layla flipped over. "After you do your homework, of course."

"Just go away."

Val sighed and got up. "Drink some tea, scribble all those feelings down in your journal, and I think you'll feel better." And that was when it struck her, a real lightbulb moment, as they say.

"Actually, Layla. Maybe you should write this person a letter. You know, tell them how you feel about what they did. I've been doing that lately, and let me tell you, it's made a world of difference."

A skeptical face peeked out from the blankets. "You want me to write a letter to the entire freshman class? I'm not doing that!"

Yikes, it really was bad. Val soldiered on. "You write in your journal all the time, right?"

"Yeah, but no one reads it!"

"And no one has to read the letter. Sometimes getting those feelings out will help you." Val made her way to the door. "It's worth trying, right?" Ugh, she sounded like Evelyn.

"Mom!"

"Okay!" Val stepped out of the room and gently shut her door.

There had been a time when she and Peter had been the topic of a rumor. She would never forget the way the boys made lewd gestures toward her and how the girls had pointed and laughed when they thought she wasn't looking.

Have sex one time as a teen, and it's suddenly all anyone could talk about. Overnight, Val's life had suddenly been defined by a few minutes spent awkwardly fumbling around in the backseat of Peter's car, for what? To feel all grown up? To say she'd done it?

Panic gripped her at the thought of the rumors surrounding Layla and Dillon being of the same nature. But surely Layla was too young for that. At least, that was what Val tried to convince herself.

Chapter 11

"**A**nd when Layla told you that happened, how did you react?" Evelyn sat across from Val on the stark white armchair, her long legs crossed at the ankles.

"Well, obviously, I wanted her to beat them to a pulp, but you've taught me that violence is not the way." She did her best to hold back a smirk, but it wasn't working. Evelyn just lifted her eyebrows and sighed.

"Okay, fine. I told her to try writing down her feelings. In the form of a letter, if you must know." God, she hated to admit that her therapist had a good idea. It was painful for sure. But Evelyn didn't give anything away.

"And how did Layla take that advice?"

Who freaking knew? Did Layla even take her advice at all? Val would consider herself lucky to have such insider knowledge into her daughter's brain, but sadly, she didn't.

"Standard response. Just yelled at me to get out of her room. Honestly, I expect nothing else."

"How is your own letter writing going?"

Now this felt like an easy share. "Amazing! I have a handful done, and that's only from the last few weeks! I'll be done in no time."

Instead of showing any sort of excitement, Evelyn's face barely shifted into a smile. "Is it important for you to finish quickly?"

"No, but I am getting them done fast. That's good, right?" Though she could tell that it wasn't. Self-improvement takes time, doesn't it?

"Tell me about them" was all Evelyn said.

Val had expected a touch more enthusiasm. She was smashing her goal, for crying out loud. "Well, I've done Peter and a couple other assholes—" Evelyn's judgment pierced through the space between them, even though her face hadn't changed. And then Val recalled the assignment Evelyn had given her during the last session. "And I took your suggestion and wrote a letter to a friend. I told her how much I loved her, you know, all the sappy shit."

Evelyn cocked her head to the side. "And how did that go?"

To Val, the process had been a little like camping: uncomfortable, exhausting, more work than it should be, but in the end, mildly satisfying. "Harder than I would have liked," she admitted.

"How about this time, you focus on writing a letter of apology?" At Val's blank expression, Evelyn continued. "Pick someone you've wronged and write a true, heartfelt apology."

Val slowly shifted her head from side to side, pondering her next assignment. She wasn't one to say she was sorry, but how hard could it be?

• • • •

ON FRIDAY, VAL SLID into the back booth of The Greasy Spoon to meet Maddie like she had promised. Bacon sizzled in the open kitchen, the glorious smell wafting into the dining area, making her stomach grumble. Barb sauntered over, and it was hard to tell which Barb she would get today. The sweet or the sour?

She flashed Barb a thousand-watt smile in an attempt to improve her chances. "Good morning, Barb, you are looking gorgeous today!" In fact, Bard looked the same as always: drab, frumpy, and eternally disappointed, but what could it hurt?

Barb greeted her with a snarl. Sour it is. Come to think of it, was Barb ever sweet to her? Maybe not.

"Don't worry, I'm getting breakfast today," Val said as Barb pulled the pencil from behind her ear. When cleaning out the hall closet, Val had discovered one of Peter's old pullovers with a wad of cash in the pocket and felt it was high time for a treat.

Barb popped a hand on her hip, her eyes still narrowed. "Damn right you are."

"I'll have a coffee and a cinnamon roll, please."

"Is that it?" Barb said as if a cinnamon roll didn't qualify as an actual breakfast. Yes, this was Boulder, but Val was not going to order the organic, free-range, egg white omelet with foraged mushrooms, thank you very much. Did this woman think she had wads of cash hidden all over her house? But really, Val should clean out more stuff, maybe there were more bundles of money in someplace Peter forgot.

The pop and sizzle of bacon grease practically called to her from the kitchen. Val stuck a finger in the air to keep Barb's attention. "And a side of bacon."

Maddie, the lifesaver that she was, sidled up next to Barb. "Oh, hi. Sorry. Excuse me." She wiggled around Barb and slid into the booth. "Good morning, so sorry I'm late," she whispered to Val.

Smiling up at Barb, Maddie said the best thing she could have said at that moment. "Hi, Barb, can I have an orange juice, coffee, and an egg sandwich, over easy, please? Oh, a stack of pancakes on the side, too?" Her eyes were all apologetic, like she shouldn't be ordering anything at all and to do so was a huge inconvenience to Barb, the one who was paid to bring out the food.

Barb's mouth did a funny thing right then. Her lips curled up, and holy shit, she was smiling. Actually smiling. Who knew a simple food order could bring out her sweet side?

"Sure, hon, I'll have that out for you soon."

"Sorry," Maddie said, turning to Val. "I cried so much last night that I forgot to eat, I guess. I woke up starving!" She had definitely dressed down today; her T-shirt was crumpled like she had pulled it from a pile on the floor. And her makeup job did little to hide her puffy, swollen eyes. Maddie had been in rougher shape than Val had thought.

"Hey," Val said, reaching a hand across the table, "never, ever apologize for eating, okay?" Or for anything else! The word "sorry" fell from her lips so easily, it was like she was apologizing for just existing.

Maddie gave her a small smile. "Thanks for meeting me today, I really needed to see a friendly face."

Ha! *Val* was the friendly face? Honestly, this girl needed to get out more.

"It's been that rough, huh?"

Maddie shrugged. "Yeah. It's going to take time, I know." She waved her hand in the air and shook her head like it was no big deal.

Barb came by with a tray of drinks, and Maddie and Val instinctively curled their fingers around their coffee mugs as if the warmth brought them comfort. Or maybe they just didn't know what to do with their hands.

"Yeesh," Maddie said after taking a sip. "Why do we come here again? The coffee is terrible, and Barb is...well, always giving you the stink eye."

"Hey." Val held up her hands. "It's walkable. From my house, your office. And it's cheap, which is priority number one for me. And Barb's good people." After weeks of mutual torment, Val had grown a soft spot for the crotchety woman. She might not enjoy putting up with Val and her skimpy orders, but Val gave her a place to direct her daily aggravation. In essence, Val was doing Barb a favor by coming here.

Maddie shrugged her acquiescence, a spot on the table capturing her attention.

Val's phone buzzed with a new text message.

Peter: *The nursing home called me. You need to go see her.*

"Ugh!" Val heaved a sigh. She dodged one of their calls and they go straight to Peter? Why had she put him down as an emergency contact in the first place?

"What?" Maddie said.

"Nothing. Peter's just all up my ass about stuff." Couldn't he just bow out of the situation? After all, she was no longer his mother-in-law, so what did he care? She hammered out a quick reply.

Val: *I'll take care of it.*

Peter: *But will you?*

Val put her phone on "do not disturb" and tossed it into her bag. She'd go and see her mother right after this and rub circles on her back until she calmed down, but she didn't have to answer to him.

"Is everything okay?" Maddie asked, her voice laced with concern.

Val waved a hand in the air. "It's fine. Are you sure you're okay?"

"I'll be fine. It's just a breakup." Though her voice wavered as she said it.

Val nodded sagely. "Time helps, sure. But it also helps to burn their stuff." Ask her how she knew.

Spluttering on a sip of coffee with horror in her eyes, Maddie managed to choke out, "What?"

"You literally burn their stuff." Val shrugged and made a face like it was obvious. "Anything burnable, anyway." She held her coffee mug up and blew on the steam. "Did Meredith leave anything behind?"

Maddie shook her head, her expression thoughtful. "I don't think so." Then her eyes brightened. "Actually, they did leave some psychology books on the shelf, but I don't think they care much about them."

Val grimaced. "No, we absolutely will not become book burners." That was not a good look for anyone. "What about a piece of mail? Or something they've given to you as a present?"

"Oh! They made me a scarf once." Maddie's eyes sparkled. "They used this glittery purple yarn that's so soft, sometimes I just rub it on my face for comfort."

"There you go. You should burn it." Val sipped her jet fuel, letting it zip into her veins.

"What? No, it's my favorite scarf!"

Their conversation stopped when Barb came back with a tray of food. Greasy eggs and delicious carbs. What better smell was there than that? She set the plates on the table in front of them.

"Thank you, Barb, you're a goddess." Val winked, and Barb returned it with a shake of her head.

Eyeing her breakfast, Val rubbed her hands together in delight. Where to start? She picked up a piece of bacon and turned her attention to Maddie.

"It may be your favorite scarf, but it was made by someone that broke your heart and crushed your spirit. Do you really want it around, bringing back memories of Meredith and the way they torpedoed your soul?" Val crunched the bacon between her teeth and had to suppress a groan. It was the perfect combination of chew and crisp. "Mmm mmm mmm, so good," she mumbled to herself. If it wasn't for the risk of clogged arteries, she would eat these delicious bad boys every day.

Maddie held up her hands. "Okay, okay, stop. I get it! I know you want me to let go, I just don't know if I'm ready yet. Besides, we're under a burn ban, I don't want to be responsible for starting a wildfire."

Here, Maddie had a point. Rainfall this summer had been lower than normal, and the heat had turned everything to kindling. If the wind was just right, a lit cigarette tossed out of a car window could start a blaze that burned hundreds of acres down in a matter of minutes. It had happened before. Val shuddered just thinking about it.

"Listen, it's just a thought. Might help with your anger."

Maddie shook her head, her brows furrowing. "I'm not angry, Val. I'm sad!"

All right, so Val was projecting. She wasn't the therapist here, she didn't know all the right things to say. If only Maddie had some better friends to go to for this crap. They ate their food in silence for a while before Val changed the subject.

"So," Val said nonchalantly. "How's the office?" She didn't want to sound too eager, but they had spent the last ten minutes focused solely on Maddie's sad relationship. That was plenty of time, right?

Maddie lifted one shoulder. "Fine, I guess."

"How's Cokehead Cari's column coming?" Yes, alliteration queen!

Maddie put her fork down and wiped her mouth with her napkin. She seemed to be bracing herself or maybe figuring out a way to say something. Finally, their eyes met, Maddie's face hard and unreadable.

"No one likes when you call her that," Maddie said.

"Oh, I doubt that very much."

"It isn't funny." Okay, maybe she was right, it wasn't funny. It was hilarious. Maddie shook her head, and her face hardened. "You know what? The office is actually a much healthier place since you left, did you know that?"

She didn't leave, she was kicked out!

"What, there are no more cookies in the breakroom, is that it? Raw veggies only? Is Sonia making everyone take the stairs?" Val rolled her eyes and made a gagging motion.

"I'm serious. Between the nicknames and the massive amounts of sarcasm you dropped everywhere, you were a bit toxic."

Val scoffed. Toxic? Sure, she had been called many things, and yes, she wasn't the greatest person to have ever lived, but toxic? This was new.

"Yes, we all loved your snickerdoodles, just not your attitude." Maddie took a swig of her orange juice as if that was where she could find bravery, set the glass down and looked Val dead in the eye. "People are nice to each other in that office now that you're gone. You constantly dished out crap. You were not the most pleasant to be around." She lifted her chin.

"And yet you hung around me. You still hang around me."

"Yeah, against my therapist's wishes." Maddie stabbed at her pancakes.

Val sat back in the booth, the coffee and overly sweet roll swirling in her gut. "Your therapist tells you not to hang out with me?" Can they even do that? She tried to picture Evelyn controlling who she spent her time with. To say that would not go over well would be quite the understatement.

Maddie sat a little straighter in her seat but refused to meet Val's eyes. "She's encouraging me to be better at setting boundaries. To spend my time with people who replenish my soul, not feed off it."

"What? I suddenly feed off your soul?"

This time, Maddie did meet her gaze. "No, you don't, but you only have breakfast with me to get dirt on the office. And even at work, you would only stop by to smack talk someone else." Her eyes softened just a bit, like she was sad. "This was the first time you asked me to meet with you because you were concerned for my well-being. Or at least I thought you were."

That same niggling in the back of her brain started up again. Val was aware of what a shitty person she was, but she didn't realize to what level. And she had never cared before. Her lips twisted with guilt. "Okay, okay, you're right. I suck. I'm sorry."

Maddie swiped at her cheek, and Val sent a wordless plea to all the nearby hippie drum circles that Maddie would not cry right now. Not here, not again.

Val reached across the table and touched Maddie's arm. "No more work talk, okay? I promise." That wasn't what Maddie needed, and right now, it was about her. "Hey, my friend is singing at The Whale this weekend. Layla will be at Peter's. Want to come with me?" Val had zero plans for actually going to this gig. The only plans she had were with her sofa and a pair of comfy pants, but the moment called for an olive branch. Although, was it still considered an olive branch if you didn't want anyone to take it?

Maddie looked dubious, but then said, "You know what? That sounds great."

Great, indeed. What did Val get for being nice? Having to put on a bra and leave the house after nine p.m., that's what.

Chapter 12

"Doing anything fun this weekend?" Val leaned against the door frame to Layla's room, eyeing the stack of dirty dishes piling up on her dresser. If Val wanted those to be cleaned, she would have to sneak them out of there and do it herself. Who knew how long that food had been adhering to the ceramic? Val was a bit surprised they didn't have mice. Or ants.

Layla sat cross-legged on her bed, putting clothes into her backpack, completely ignoring Val's presence. As usual. Her hair was corralled in a ponytail, and the loose cotton shirt she wore dangled off one shoulder, bra strap on full display. The sight of her looking so grown up made Val's heart skip a beat. It was easy to imagine how Layla might change over the next few years and how she might look when she was a full-fledged adult, and it was almost heartbreaking.

Val stepped into the room ever so slightly, careful not to disturb any junk on the floor. "What do you and your dad have planned for the weekend?" she asked again, hoping for an answer this time.

"God, Mom, I don't know!"

It was like Val was the only person in the world who had the power to press Layla's annoyance button, and she inadvertently tripped it whenever she opened her mouth. Being a teen was hard, but Val certainly wasn't this snippy when she was growing up, was she? Not that her mom had been around to hear it.

"Are you visiting friends, having any sleepovers?" Val asked this in her most nonchalant voice, as if it didn't matter what Layla's answer was, when really Val was screaming inside, *Please don't have sex!*

Layla stopped what she was doing and hurled a glare at Val so hard, it compelled her to take a giant step back. And then Layla's face changed. She smiled, the kind of smile you don't want to see on your child. Arrogant, manipulative. Scary, even.

"Fine," Layla said, sitting up a bit straighter. "Since you asked. Remember Dillon? From the mall?"

This guy again? Val shrugged as casually as she could. "Vaguely."

"I'm going to his house."

"Oh?" Val absently brushed a crumb off Layla's comforter, pretending to be listening but not completely invested.

"Yeah." Layla crossed her arms over her chest, the picture of defiance. "And we're going to sneak into his dad's liquor cabinet, invite some people over, and probably end the night with an orgy. Is that what you wanted to hear?"

"Jesus, Layla!" Val covered her face with her hands. That was an image she didn't need. One that no parent needed. Did she even know what an orgy was? It certainly wasn't covered in Val and Peter's sex talks.

"What? You keep pestering me about it!" Layla smiled for real this time, balled up a T-shirt and hurled it at Val's face. "Dad and I are probably just going to watch a movie tonight and order some pizza."

Val's heart twisted. Family movie night had always been Val's idea. It was her thing. And Layla hadn't been interested in that for a while, but now she was going to do that with her dad. Trying to keep the disappointment off her face, Val just nodded and tossed the T-shirt onto the bed.

"We have a group project for history class that's due in a couple of weeks, so a few people are coming over, and we'll be working on that tomorrow," Layla said as she shoved the shirt into her backpack without bothering to fold it.

These were probably the most words Layla had spoken to her in weeks, and Val didn't want her to stop. She crept farther into the room. "So your dad will make sure there are plenty of condoms for this orgy of yours?"

"Ew, Mom! God, I was just kidding about that."

Val found an empty spot on the bed and sat down. "I know that we're both kidding. However—"

Layla held up her hands before she could continue. "No, we're not having another sex talk! Oh, my god, just get out."

Val patted her on the knee and stood. "I just want you to be safe, that's all."

Layla heaved a sigh. "You worry too much."

But if Val didn't worry, who would? Peter spent so much time on breathing exercises, she wasn't sure he was capable of the emotion.

"Well, have a fun weekend. I'll see you after school on Monday, okay?"

Layla made her best "duh" face and continued to pack her bag.

"I'm off to meet with friends," Val said as if Layla had asked about her plans for the evening. "Rupa's playing tonight."

Layla made a face that said, "like I care."

"Your dad should be here soon." Val blew her a kiss. "I love you!"

"Go away!"

Chapter 13

"Hey! I'm so glad you could make it!" Rupa threw her arms around Val and squeezed, the scent of her cinnamon and orange body spray wafting up. The Whale usually smelled of stale beer, so it was a bit of a delicious shock to her senses.

Val pulled away and held her at arm's length to take in this new and improved version of Rupa. Her hair had been curled and pinned to the side, elegant waves draped over one shoulder. She wore high-waisted black pants that hugged her curvy hips just right, and a sleeveless, turquoise top that popped against her dark brown skin. Paired with strappy black sandals and gold hoop earrings, she was a bombshell.

"You look incredible," Val said. Rupa cocked her hip and cupped a hand around her ear at the compliment, clearly waiting for more. Val laughed and shouted for all nearby patrons to hear, "You look hot as hell!"

At this, Rupa fanned her face and acted like she had never heard such a statement before. Hardly. This woman was so hot, she had admirers everywhere she went. And she knew it.

"I'm trying something new." Rupa gave Val the once-over and added, "Wouldn't hurt for you to do the same. Do you even look in the mirror before you leave the house?"

"What are you talking about?" Incredulous, Val inspected the old Cranberries T-shirt she wore for any new stains or holes but found nothing major. "This is vintage!" She sent Rupa a playful scowl and gave the worn cotton a protective caress.

With a dubious expression, Rupa adjusted her mic stand. "I wouldn't give it that much credit."

Val scoffed. "Hey, T-shirts are sexy."

"You look like an old white guy."

Whatever. It wasn't like she was on the prowl tonight. She wasn't here to pick anyone up, she was here for Maddie. And just as she thought it, Maddie entered the bar.

"Now that's what I'm talking about!" Rupa said as Maddie strutted over to them, her slinky black dress hitting her mid-thigh and making her long legs go on forever.

"Jesus," Val murmured. Maddie towered above the crowd in a pair of red heels, her shoulders back and head held high. She was unrecognizable.

Val made introductions, and Rupa gushed over Maddie's shoes. Maddie's face turned crimson at the attention, and just when Val thought she might crumple in on herself and apologize for something, she just shrugged and said, "Meredith didn't like to go out. I haven't been out in a year if you can believe that."

"You need to give Val some pointers on how to dress for a night out," Rupa said. "You'd think she hasn't been out in years."

Well, it was true, Val hadn't been out in a while, but not because anyone was keeping her at home. She just preferred her cozy sofa and a pair of pajamas to a cold, steel barstool.

"Hey," Val said to her two friends. "Fuck you both." She punctuated her statement with her middle fingers. "I'm going to grab a drink, what can I get you?"

Rupa waved her off. "I'm good." She picked up a full pint glass from a nearby chair and held it up.

Val turned to Maddie. "What'll it be, hot stuff?"

She scrunched up her face and rubbed at the back of her neck. "Hmm. I don't know. Whatever you're having?"

"Maddie, you don't even know what I'm going to order."

Maddie blushed, and her gaze hit the floor. "I guess I just drank whatever Meredith did."

"Which was...?"

"Beer mostly." Maddie shrugged.

This was brutal. "Maddie, do you like beer?"

She pursed her lips and shook her head. "Not really."

Either Meredith did a number on her or Maddie's people-pleasing instincts were off the charts. Val shoved her hands into her pockets to keep from grabbing Maddie and shaking her senseless. "No beer, then. Any idea what you do like?"

"Something fruity, maybe?"

Finally, she could work with that. "Got it. Grab us a table, will you?"

The floor was sticky, the soles of her slip-on sneakers ripped like Velcro with every step as she made her way up to the bar.

"What can I get you?" the bartender asked as Val studied the taps. What was she in the mood for tonight? Chocolate pistachio stout? Honey lavender lager? Colorado might be home to some amazing craft breweries, but the flavor combinations they came up with grew more wild with each passing day.

"How about a Fat Tire?" Val said. Nothing wrong with a good old standby. "And something fruity for my friend over there." She gestured to Maddie, who had found a table far enough away from the speakers to not blow out their eardrums but close enough to see the band. "Whatever you recommend for a rough breakup."

The bartender, a tall kid with a Pee-Wee Herman face, just shrugged. "Uh, I don't know."

"Just pour the beer, I got this."

And there was Gina, the very cute, muscled bartender who sent a zing up Val's spine. She winked at Val and filled a tumbler with ice, her movements so quick and precise Val could hardly tell what she put in it. Gina set it on the counter and said, "Vodka cranberry. Works wonders."

Her golden brown skin shone against the white T-shirt she wore. A gold chain dangled from her neck and dipped just below where the neckline had been torn in, confirming what Val had said all along: T-shirts were sexy. Very sexy.

Val raised her eyebrows, a smile pulling at the corner of her mouth. "Does it now? Good to know." She paid for the drinks, and Gina offered her a flirty smile before turning to help the next customer. The bar had filled up quickly; Val had to weave her way through the crowd, holding her drinks steady.

"I want to warn you," Val shouted to be heard over the din, setting the vodka cranberry in front of Maddie. "Too many of these and you'll be on the floor. So take it slow, okay?" Val had never had the pleasure of seeing Maddie drunk, and while Maddie could probably use a night of debauchery, Val wasn't up for babysitting.

"Thanks, Val." Maddie met Val's gaze and shook her head. "For the drink, but really for getting me out of the house. I didn't know how much I needed this." Maddie's smile was wide and bright, and something tugged at Val's heart.

The blaring screech of the amp saved her from her feelings, and the entire room collectively covered their ears.

"Sorry, friends," Rupa's melodious voice soothed into the microphone. Her bandmates made some adjustments behind her, and soon enough, the guitar began a smooth rhythmic strum.

"Thank you so much for coming out to see us tonight! We are Absurdity in Motion." Rupa looked out over the crowd, catching Val's eye. She winked. Her stage presence was unbelievable. The music moved through her, and she belted out the lyrics as easy as breathing, as if she needed to sing as much as she needed air. Rupa's voice sang out over the crowd, giving Val goose bumps.

Their music was eclectic, and let's say, not for everyone. At times, they sounded very indie rock, and others more folksy, and sometimes downright weird. It didn't matter, though. Val was always in awe of her performances. She would gladly see them more often if they ever occurred during daylight hours.

It only took one song for Maddie to pound back her drink. "I'm going to get another, do you want anything?" Maddie asked.

Val held up her pint, nearly three-quarters full, and shook her head. If Maddie kept this up, she would be in a world of hurt. But then again, if gulping down vodka cranberries cheered her up, who was Val to get in the way?

A few minutes later, Maddie sauntered back with a full tumbler in hand. She dropped a business card on the table. "This is from the bartender," she said with a knowing smile.

"You got Pee-Wee Herman's phone number?" Val slapped the table in feigned surprise.

Maddie scrunched her face. "Who?"

That would take ages to explain, and how could one even describe the late eighties' phenomenon without being branded a weirdo?

"Never mind." Val inspected the card. On the front was The Whale's logo and generic contact info, but scrawled across the back was a phone number and the name Gina. She forced her disappointment down. Why should she care? Maddie could get any phone number she wanted. Val wasn't interested in Gina, anyway.

"Val!" Maddie waved her hand in front of Val's face. "It's for you, dummy. Ask her out."

Okay, maybe she was interested in Gina. "Right! Thank you?" Val stuffed the card into her pocket and ignored the tickle of possibility that fluttered in her belly.

· · · ·

FOUR VODKA CRANBERRIES later, and Maddie was done for the night. That was all it took for Maddie to flirt with everyone, stumble over chairs, spill her drink, and giggle like she had just drawn dicks on the faces of her sleeping frenemies. It was embarrassing. Either Gina had been pouring doubles or Maddie was a severe lightweight. And Val wasn't the only one who noticed. Rupa, who had been playing gigs in bars for over twenty years, started giving Val "the look." The get-your-friend-out-of-here-before-she-ruins-my-set look. Val did not hesitate.

"Hey, Mad, it's getting late. How about we get you home, huh?" Val collected the contents of Maddie's purse that she had drunkenly emptied onto the table in search of lip balm. Val threw it all back in and hooked Maddie's elbow to lift her up.

"Oh, I don't want to go home!" Maddie's voice was whiny, and Val hadn't consumed enough alcohol to deal with that. Val was out of the house after her bedtime at a very loud bar filled with people having fun, and it was getting annoying.

"I know you don't want to, sweetie, but we all need to get to sleep." Val used her best motherly voice, the one she used when Layla was four and vehemently rejected her bedtime.

"But I'm not tired!" God, drunks and kids were one and the same, weren't they?

"Oh, honey, give it five minutes." Val steered the tall, tipsy Maddie out of the bar, giving Gina a little salute. She sighed. Another lifetime ago, and she would have been all over that. Now she was just too old and too tired.

When they stumbled out onto the sidewalk, Val pulled Maddie's phone out of her purse and handed it to her. "Let's call you an Uber, okay?"

"Yup." Maddie swayed on her feet and jabbed at her phone screen. Val held on to her arm to keep her upright. Grunting, Maddie handed the phone back. "Hmm. I can't."

Val sighed, shoved Maddie's phone back into her purse, pulled her own out of her back pocket, and swiped up the ride share app. "What's your address?" Maddie just giggled in response. Crap, Val didn't know where Maddie lived, how could she get her home?

"All right, you can sleep on my couch, you drunk giant. But we have to walk." It was the most brutal six blocks Val had trudged. They stopped halfway so Maddie could transfer the contents of her stomach into a very unfortunate bush and then had to backtrack to find the shoes she'd taken off in order to do so. Val rejoiced when they finally made it to the tiny house.

She inserted the key just so, gave it a wiggle, and pushed against the door with all her might. They barreled into the house together. One of these days, she was going to get someone to fix the damned thing.

She steered Maddie down the hall and ordered her to use the bathroom while she made up the sleeper sofa. Once Maddie passed out, Val got ready for bed and made a cup of tea. Her brain was wired from the noisy bar, the bass still thumping in her head. Between that and the mom part of her brain that worried about Maddie choking on her own vomit, there was no way she would sleep comfortably tonight. Settling into the cozy armchair that she often used for reading, she draped a throw blanket across her lap and opened her laptop. Might as well do some work while she watched over the adult-sized baby.

Maddie, splayed out like a dead body, her mouth wide open, had snores that were soft and rhythmic, like a human sound machine. It was sweet, really. Maddie was annoying sometimes, but it wasn't her fault. She just needed someone to care for her. Meredith hadn't cared, Val typically didn't care. Who was looking out for Maddie? She certainly didn't have the confidence to do that for herself. Yet.

Val might have encouraged Maddie to abandon her pity party for one night, but Val also got out of the house. It didn't end like she thought it would, but she'd take the win. Bathing in Rupa's sensuous melodies, socializing with friends, hell, Val even flirted tonight! A feat in itself! It was quite possible that Maddie had climbed the ladder from a person Val barely tolerated to maybe a friend.

Feeling so inspired, Val opened her document of letters and let her fingers fly across the keyboard.

Dear Maddie,

I remember your first day at Mile High Magazine. *You were timid and shy but somehow full of pep and cheer. You were over the moon to work with Sonia, like we all were. Because, let's face it, she's a powerhouse! But you carried with you this inability to believe in yourself, and I just couldn't stand it. That might be why I walked all over you—because you let me.*

That wasn't an apology, was it? She deleted the last part and tried again.

Back in the office, I took advantage of your need to please people, and I walked all over you. I was the one stealing your yogurt. And the past few months, I've been using you. I've been so focused on getting my job back, I ignored your struggles. You were an exceptional friend to me, regardless. You didn't deserve any of that, and I certainly don't deserve you. I'm so sorry.

There was suddenly a weight in her chest. Val moved to close the laptop. Too many feelings were cropping up, and she couldn't handle it. But when she glanced in Maddie's direction, it was Evelyn she pictured. Perched on the edge of the sofa, her back ramrod straight, legs crossed at the ankles. She didn't even have to say anything, her expression said it all. Val could do this. She took a deep breath and continued.

Somewhere along the way, you grew on me. You even picked up a hot chick's phone number for me tonight when you could have had it all to yourself. You selfless little minx.

You need to know that you are worthy of love. Don't let people like Meredith cut you down or hold you back. You were beautiful and confident tonight, albeit a little drunk, but you carried yourself like someone who mattered. It was a sight to behold.

I still find you annoying as hell sometimes, but thank you for being you. The world needs more of your positive sunshine.

The anvil in her chest grew heavier, and tears sprang to her eyes. If she knew apologizing would make her weepy, she wouldn't have done it. Val quickly swiped at her eyes and shook her head. She couldn't be sure if it was the booze, the sappy letter, or the sheer exhaustion that had crept in, but she didn't like it, whatever it was. Was this what it felt like to be sentimental? She shuddered at the thought.

There was no way she could sleep when she felt so out of balance. Thankfully, she knew just the thing to help. She entered down to start a new line and typed furiously.

Dear Ninth Grade Dipshits,

My daughter is the coolest person you will ever meet. An artist, full of amazing ideas, brimming with witty sarcasm. You'd be the luckiest kids alive to know her. But I'm not sure you even deserve to.

Val's eyes filled with tears again. Maybe this wasn't such a good idea. Boozy and emotional was a dangerous combo. The only thing to cure this strange vulnerability was anger. Quick, quick, what made her blood pressure rise? If only she could tap into it, she could settle into herself and go to sleep.

She channeled her annoyance and let her fingers do the talking. Her front door and its inability to open, the stupid little plant on her windowsill that never enjoyed whatever amount of water Val gave it, and to her bank account for being so goddamn empty.

There. Instant relief. The anvil was gone and so were the tears. And she was almost halfway to her goal. She needed to sleep before she hammered out all her forty letters in one night. Evelyn would balk at the quality. She certainly wasn't putting in the effort to really make any self-improvements, but it was a start, right? She pushed the laptop onto the coffee table, clicked the light off, and snuggled into her big chair.

Chapter 14

"Ugh."

Val woke to Maddie's hungover murmurs, her body stiff. She stretched, instantly regretting her decision to sleep in that stupid chair. Her joints popped as she moved, and the muscle along the side of her neck screamed from being scrunched the entire night. Sitting up as gingerly as she could, Val rolled her head from side to side, letting out a groan herself.

Maddie sat up, her hair spiked out in all directions, a red mark covering half her face where it had been smashed into the pillow. She was a wreck.

"Good morning, sunshine," Val said. "How are you feeling?"

"Meh" was all she got in response.

"Drink some water." Val gestured to the giant glass she left on the coffee table last night. "I'm going to make you some coffee and eggs, gotta soak up all that vodka you had last night."

Val made her way into the kitchen, shaking out her stiff legs. There was a rustling of sheets and more moaning coming from the living room. Val laughed and thanked the gods that she didn't have more than two drinks. Hangovers were definitely for the young. She was too old for that shit. Maddie probably was, too.

Waiting for the pan to heat and the coffee to perk, Val brought her phone to life. She opened up her text chain with Layla and sent her a good morning GIF of a squirrel stretching its teeny tiny arms to the sky. These used to make Layla squeal with delight at the cuteness of it all. Maybe she'd still find it adorable. After a few moments of no reply, Val closed the text window and sighed. She was probably still sleeping, up late watching a movie with her dad. Val did her best not to be jealous and focused on making breakfast.

By the time Val made it back out to the living room, Maddie had turned the bed back into the sofa, the blankets folded and stacked neatly on the coffee table. Maddie was sitting on the floor, Val's laptop in front of her face, her eyes wide.

"Val, what is this?" Maddie said in a scratchy voice. She looked like she was concentrating hard, trying to place something.

"What are you doing?" Val set the tray of food down as quickly as she could without spilling it everywhere and grabbed the laptop, snapping it shut. Maddie couldn't have seen anything too bad, could she? "Do you always snoop?"

"I wasn't snooping, I just bumped the coffee table when I made the bed, and there was my name on the screen. I couldn't *not* look!" Maddie stared at Val, and Val couldn't tell if she was angry or genuinely curious. "What was that? You wrote a letter to me? And to inanimate objects? What's going on?"

It was too early to get into an argument, and Val didn't want to anyway. "Fine. Don't laugh, okay?"

Maddie held up her hands. "You saw me make an ass out of myself last night. What do I have to laugh about?"

Fair point. Val heaved a sigh and told her all about her therapy and the letters Evelyn assigned her to write. "I'm sort of taking it on as a challenge. You know, I turned forty this year and...I don't know."

"Wait. Let me get this right. You're taking a therapy assignment and turning it into an exercise in self-improvement?" Maddie became more animated with every word, even though she had to have been clouded by sleepiness and the after-effects of booze. It was like she was impressed or something.

"Well, I guess." This was embarrassing. Val hadn't even told Rupa yet, and that wouldn't matter because she would know what Val was trying to accomplish. But telling Maddie made her uncomfortable. They weren't at this stage in their friendship for this, were they? Val waved her off. "I don't even know why I'm doing it. It sounds so stupid, I know."

Maddie shook her head. "Writing letters of gratitude and owning up to your mistakes doesn't sound stupid at all. I think it's admirable. I mean, I don't know why you're so mad at your plant, but—"

Val waved her hand in the air. "Just getting my feelings down, that's all."

"Actually..." Maddie sat up straighter, and her eyes brightened. "This is a great idea!"

Val handed her a cup of coffee from the tray and shrugged. "Thanks?"

Maddie shook her head. "No, this is a great idea for the magazine! You could get your column back with this!"

Confusion set in. How? Val wrote hard-hitting pieces, not self-improvement drivel. Besides, *Mile High Magazine* wasn't like *Cosmo*. Feelings weren't a feature.

Maddie must have read her mind because she piped up. "I know what you're thinking." She put the coffee on the table and talked excitedly, her hands waving about with every word she said. "I didn't tell you this because I know it would have pissed you off, but the board has asked Sonia to steer away from any controversial topics and focus more on positive content that readers can connect with on an emotional level. Something about the news always being a big downer, people don't want to read it anymore."

Val was hardly listening. When had they decided to do this? They were phoning it in and churning out fluff because people were too sensitive to deal with cold, hard facts?

"They're not wrong. Think about it. A column dedicated to your journey of self-improvement!" Maddie's eyes went wide as the idea occurred to her, like she was plotting her next piece right there on the spot. "We could print your letters, and the readers could go on the journey with you. *Join Valerie Knight on her journey of gratitude, forgiveness, and self-improvement.* Oh, my gosh, Sonia is going to love it!" She dug her phone from her purse and swiped at the screen.

"First off," Val said, intent on squashing this idea like a bug, "please stop calling it a journey. I'm right here, I'm not on some freaking adventure. It's not a road trip, I'm not sailing around the world. I'm just here trying to keep my Wi-Fi connected."

Maddie wasn't listening, her eyes were lit up with excitement, her thumbs flying over the keyboard.

"Second," Val said, "no one said anything about forgiveness." Crap, did she just jinx it? Was Evelyn going to make forgiveness her next assignment?

"Trust me. We've been brainstorming a new direction for the column since..." Maddie glanced up at Val, her eyebrows drawn together. Then she waved her hand in the air and smiled. "Never mind. I just know this is going to get your column back! You have to pitch it to her!"

Of course Maddie had said wild things before, but this was straight up bananas. Val couldn't publish these letters. Not any of the ones she had written, anyway. The magazine wasn't allocated that many F words in their publication. Sure, maybe she could get her column back, but then she'd have to open her emotional vault for the public, and she could barely open it for herself.

"I know you think this is a great idea, but—"

Before Val had a chance to finish the sentence, Maddie was off the floor, her hand over her mouth, racing down the hall. Val sent a silent plea to the goddess of clean bathrooms that she made it to the toilet in time.

Chapter 15

"Hey, Mom, I brought someone to see you," Val said in a soft voice as she entered her mother's room. There was no tantrum to deal with today, no broken glass, or traumatized orderlies. Just another regular day of her mother not knowing her.

Her mother's hunched body had withered down to bone since the last time Val had been there. So frail, she was practically swallowed by an overstuffed armchair. She didn't look up when Val walked in, just stared at the hands in her lap.

"Hey, Lulu," Layla said with a smile.

Val hadn't wanted to bring her here to her weekly visit with her mother. Not only did she not want Layla to witness her grandmother's decline in this way, but she didn't want Layla to see Val flounder as a daughter. This was just facetime, putting in the bare minimum that the professionals suggest and nothing more. But Layla had insisted, certain that she could put a smile on the old woman's face. Val briefly wondered if Layla smuggled in the fixings for a martini because that would certainly do it.

Her mother's face lit up at the sight of Layla, her features softening. Worry replaced with relief, joy even.

"Oh, Valerie," she said, reaching up to touch Layla's cheek.

"Mom, that's Layla, your granddaughter. Remember?"

"It's okay. The doctor said to just play along. I can do that," Layla whispered in Val's direction.

"My sweet Valerie. Where have you been?" Her mother smiled, the only worry in her eyes strictly maternal. When was the last time she looked at Val that way? Had she ever been concerned for Val's well-being? Surely, she must have been, but Val had a hard time remembering.

"I'm right here," Layla said, patting her hand.

Her mom swiped at a stray tear, a smile of pride and love written all over her face, and Val couldn't help the twinge of something she couldn't name, didn't want to name. To see the adoration her mother had directed at her daughter that had never been for her was hard to take.

"How about some fresh sheets, Mom?" Val said, eyeing the rumpled bed. She needed to keep her hands busy, her mind busy so she didn't worry about all the things: Layla growing up too fast, getting her job back, and paying for this obnoxiously expensive facility. Changing the sheets? That she could do.

When Val made her way out of the bedroom, a ball of bed linens in her hands, the sight of Layla and her mom stopped her short.

Layla had maneuvered the food tray in between the two of them, and with a gentle, practiced hand, she glided nail polish onto her mother's fingernails. And before Val could analyze the sudden hot sting behind her eyes and the vise gripping her chest, she recalled that yes, the only other thing that could make her mom happier than a fancy cocktail was a trip to the salon. How could she have forgotten?

"Come on, Layla, it's time to go."

"Almost done," she said, painting the last nail before capping the bottle. "It was good to see you, Lulu." She smiled at the old woman.

"Wait! I...I have something for you," her mom said. But then a shadow crossed over her face as if struggling to remember what it was.

Val sucked in a breath. They needed to get out of here before this turned into a whole thing, and she was stuck rubbing her mom's back to calm her down.

She knelt in front of her mother and placed a hand on her arm. "Mom, we'll find that next time I'm here, okay?"

Her mom scrunched her eyebrows together, not fully convinced, but instead of spiraling into confusion, she just nodded.

And they left her mom fiddling with her fingers in her armchair, and Val balled up the guilt that eased its way into her heart and kicked it as far away as she could.

Chapter 16

The door chimed as Val waltzed into The Greasy Spoon the next morning. Quiet chatter filled the air, and the sweet, yeasty smell of fresh cinnamon rolls wafted through the dining room. Val flashed Barb her most dazzling smile and sauntered back to their usual spot in the corner. Right before she could toss her bag onto the vinyl booth, her gaze landed on them. People. A couple with a small child, to be exact. Sitting at her table.

Val spun around and surveyed the room. Of all the places to sit, this couple had to choose the only booth? Her booth? A booth gave much needed privacy so she could work without someone looking over her shoulder or talk about certain people without anyone overhearing. And now she'd have to choose a table in the center of the room. To just sit out in the open. Exposed. Was she being dramatic? Maybe.

With hands on hips, Barb eyed Val from the opposite side of the room. If only the door didn't have such an obnoxious bell, she could have sneaked in, and maybe Barb wouldn't have noticed her until Maddie arrived. For whatever reason, Barb loved Maddie. She would trip over her orthopedic clown shoes to bring her whatever her heart desired but could only offer Val dirty looks.

Val reluctantly plopped her bag on the closest table and sat down. There was no sinking into the chair or slouching in the seat. Unlike the booth cushions, which had been worn down with so much give that one could probably sleep on them, the chairs were hard and uncomfortable. Val grumbled to herself. It had been over a week since their night at The Whale, and Val was itching to get an update on the office, but now she was in a foul mood.

"Let me guess, just coffee." Barb's voice boomed next to her, jolting Val out of her thoughts.

Val placed a hand on her chest. "Jesus, Barb! You scared the crap out of me." Barb could easily moonlight at a haunted house. As herself.

She didn't even blink. "Just coffee?"

"Oh, no." Val laughed. "Don't sell yourself short like that. What you serve is more than 'just' coffee. In one cup of your special brew, I can taste the fiery notes of scorched earth and hear the shriek of thousands of animals who've lost the canopy in which they live. It's more than 'just coffee,' it's deforestation in a cup."

Barb grunted and stalked over to a neighboring table.

"But yes, coffee, please," Val called after her.

Val whipped open her laptop and pulled up her most recent article on how local beauty pageants were sexualizing young girls. She had spent the last two weeks researching the crap out of it, but now that she was finally sitting down to write it, she was getting tripped up on her words. And it was tough writing on this subject without invoking JonBenet Ramsey. Boulder had been famous for the 1996 murder of the six-year-old beauty queen, but it didn't want to be. And Val really didn't want to be the one to bring it back up.

The screen stared blankly back at her, mocking her inability to formulate a coherent sentence. Would Sonia even want this anyway? Was this too hard hitting and controversial now?

Startling her out of her writer's block, Maddie launched herself into the seat across from her. The mischievous smile she had on gave Val pause. Maddie was up to something, and it couldn't be good.

"Guess who I ran into?" she said, her voice all coy and sing-songy.

Val had no interest in guessing and quite frankly didn't give a shit. "I don't know, your mailman?"

Maddie laughed. "Why would you care if I ran into my mailman?" Exactly. She wouldn't. "And the proper term is letter carrier or mail carrier because you don't have to be a man to do it. Come on, Val, it's not the nineties anymore."

"The nineties?" Val's voice rose an octave. "Wait, you were alive in the nineties, right?" Maybe Maddie was younger than Val had originally thought. Had she been an intern when she started at the magazine? Was Val an ancient dinosaur?

"Ha! You're so funny." This didn't make her feel any better.

Barb made her appearance next to the table, still glowering. "Coffee," she said, setting down a mug in front of Val. She turned her attention to Maddie, her voice a little less irritated. "What can I get you, hon?" Hon? Since when did Barb use affectionate nicknames? And where was hers?

"Hmm." Maddie looked over the menu as if she didn't already know what they offered, as if it had magically morphed into an artisanal breakfast since last Tuesday and they were serving up anything other than greasy diner fare.

"How about a stack of pancakes and..." Maddie flipped the menu around and back again, her lips pursed. "Do you have chai?"

"No." Barb's tone made it sound like serving anything other than this sludge every morning would be a criminal offense. It was thick and bitter, but Val didn't mind. It was cheap and served as a vehicle for getting caffeine into her veins. She didn't need it to be fancy, locally roasted, or eight freaking dollars a cup.

"Coffee, then. Thank you!" Maddie gave Barb a genuine smile and handed her the menu. She turned her attention back to Val.

"Anyway, who did you run into?" Val asked.

"Oh, right!" The playfulness returned to her eyes, and she sat forward in the booth, leaning her elbows on the table. She peered at Val over her laptop and waggled her eyebrows, as if waiting for Val to pick up where they left off and keep guessing. "I'll give you a hint. She is gorgeous."

Deciding to play her little game just this once, Val shut her laptop and scooted it out of the way. She put her elbows on the table and mirrored Maddie's posture. "Gorgeous like Sofía Vergara or Cara Delevingne?"

"Cara Delevingne, for sure." Maddie's shoulders did a little shimmy.

Tapping her chin, Val said, "Was it...Cara Delevingne?"

"Oh, come on, you're not even trying."

Val sat back and folded her arms over her chest. "I give up, who did you run into?"

In the same way one might yell "surprise!" Maddie threw her hands in the air and said, "Gina!"

Val's brain flipped through its old Rolodex of people she knew and landed on the hot bartender. Her cheeks heated, recalling the unusual level of attraction Val had felt. And the flirting. Oh, god, the flirting. She wanted to hide her face in her hands and melt into a pile of hot humiliation right there in the middle of the diner. Instead, she shrugged and said, "Who's Gina?"

Clearly this was the wrong thing to say. Maddie's shoulders slumped in obvious disappointment. "You know, Gina!" As if saying her name again would magically conjure up her face.

Val just shook her head and pretended like she didn't recognize the name and that the warmth in her chest meant nothing.

"The bartender. The hottie from the other night?"

"Oh, right," Val said, not very convincingly. "That Gina."

Maddie seemed to be searching Val's face for something, so she did her best to smile. It didn't work.

"I gave you her number! You haven't reached out? What is wrong with you?" Maddie's face fell.

Dating wasn't in the cards for Val at the moment. She had to focus. On getting her job back and keeping her mother cared for. And there was always Layla to worry about. She didn't have the time or energy to date. Plus, dating was expensive. Always going out and buying fancy foods, doing stuff that cost money. It was honestly too much.

But she didn't have the patience to tell any of this to Maddie. She just shrugged.

"She was really hoping you would text her." As if Maddie were concerned about her well-being. Aw, Val should be touched.

"Can't please everyone," Val said lamely and took a sip of her coffee, the sludge coating her tongue and scorching her throat. She gestured to herself. "I'm a mess, Maddie. I'm not dateable at the moment."

Maddie waved a hand in front of her face and shook her head. "You're no more a mess than the rest of us." She looked at Val with huge, caring eyes. Val just stared back. This wasn't the same Maddie who had sobbed into her pancakes or the one who barfed all over Val's bathroom rug.

"Who are you and what have you done with Maddie?"

Laughing, Maddie said, "I know! I am a different person, I can feel it." She shrugged.

Val eyed her skeptically. "You didn't join laughing yoga, did you?" The fools who stood around and laughed in each other's faces for a half hour were truly losing their minds. Maddie huffed a laugh and shook her head. "All right, you joined a cult. Which one? Maybe I can write an article about that. Ooh! It can be called *How I Tore My Friend from the Hands of a Local Cult*. Sonia would love that."

"No! I didn't join a cult or do that weird yoga. Oh, but I do want to try goat yoga. Can you believe I haven't done that yet? I mean, it's been here for years, and I only go to visit the goats when it's baby time. Oh, my gosh, those baby goats are just the cutest, aren't they?"

Val snapped her fingers in front of Maddie's face. "Mad! I don't give a shit about the goats, okay?"

"Right, fine. Anyway, I just, I don't know, woke up feeling like everything was going to be okay. Meredith is gone, but it's okay. I'm going to be okay." And for whatever reason, Val believed her. "And you'll be okay, too."

"I am okay. I'm fine. Just not interested in dating, that's all." Orgasms? Sure. Dating? Not so much.

Barb returned and plopped the order of food on the table. She gave Val the stink eye before turning away.

TWENTY MINUTES AND a stack of pancakes later, Maddie wiped her face with a napkin and packed up her stuff. "I've got to head to the office." She pulled out her wallet and flung a twenty-dollar bill on the table. Val did a quick calculation to see if it would cover her coffee and tip, but no dice.

"Tell those fuckers 'hi' from me." Val opened her laptop back up, ready to dive into her article.

Maddie stopped what she was doing. "Oh, have you given any more thought to what we talked about?"

Val squinched her face up. "I'm not ready to date, I told you that."

"No, your letters."

"Right. Those things." Val had considered it, but she didn't have any worth showing Sonia at this point, at least nothing they would even think of printing. She would need to craft some letters that were poignant, emotional, moving somehow. And right now, she just didn't have that.

"I don't know. I don't think Sonia would be up for that. And I don't know if I want to put that sort of personal information out there."

Maddie rolled her eyes. "Puh-lease. You wrote an entire article about your personal trip on mushrooms when the psychedelic measure hit the ballot. How would this be any different?"

"Because it's not just me, these are letters to real people. Hell, *you* are one of those people. How would you feel about that getting put in the magazine?"

"Change the names. We have to do that all the time to protect people's privacy."

"Yeah, but—"

"Who wouldn't want to read about you getting your life together?"

"Getting my life together? Geez, Maddie, I might have some stuff to work on, but I'm not a complete dumpster fire."

"The readers will love it. Sonia will love it!" Maddie's big brown eyes were bright and pleading. "You won't know until you try."

"If I say I'll think about it, will you leave it alone?"

"Fine."

"Okay, I'll think about it," she lied.

"Be quick, though, we're working with a deadline here!" She gave Val a soft smile and slung her messenger bag over her shoulder.

Val steered her attention to her beauty pageant article, in hopes that inspiration had struck. But when Barb towered over her a few minutes later, she still hadn't typed any more words.

"This isn't a Starbucks," Barb said, a hand on her large hip. Her hard face sported a deep scowl, and Val absently wondered if she'd been getting enough fiber in her diet.

She stood there and glared at Val like she was an unwelcome bug; no matter how many times you swatted it with a rolled-up magazine, the little pest just wouldn't die.

"This isn't a Starbucks," Barb said again when Val didn't answer, this time loud enough for the whole place to hear.

Val shook her head and inspected her coffee mug. "You don't say." She imagined Barb would rather impale herself than serve up a pumpkin spice latte.

Barb heaved a constipated sigh. "You can't just park it here all day."

"It's not like this place is teeming with people looking for a place to sit." Val gestured around the diner. Her booth was still taken by the whiny child and its overlords, while a couple of tables in the center were occupied with hungover college students. It wasn't exactly a busy day.

"You can go somewhere else for free Wi-Fi."

"And then I wouldn't get to soak in your rays of sunshine," Val said as she shoved her laptop in her bag. "But fine, I'll go." She briefly considered ordering a cinnamon roll, just to get a chance to finish her article, but that also came with a high probability that it would come back covered in someone's spit.

Chapter 17

"Your mother will have to be relocated to a different facility by the end of the month if you're unable to keep up with the payments." Val had been cleaning up breakfast dishes that Monday morning when the nursing home called for the third time.

The woman from the billing department had been compassionate and understanding in the first few messages she left, but this one was harsh. By now, Val owed them thousands of dollars that she just didn't have. It didn't matter if she eased up on grocery spending, cut back on her coffees out with Maddie, or canceled the one and only streaming service they'd hung on to, it wouldn't be enough.

And the time she spent agonizing over word choice in her articles had been fruitless. She needed to face the facts, she wasn't getting her job back. She'd need to go out and get something else. The *Now Hiring* sign in the Whole Foods window flashed through her mind. Great, the worst had come. A green apron and kombucha-drinking hippies.

As she was about to spin into a whirlpool of self-pity, Val's phone pinged with a new text, and her heart stopped for a tiny beat.

Sonia: *Come in today, we need to talk.*

No way. Sonia must have loved her take on the beauty pageants. Yes! This was it! She was going to get her column back. She could finally buy the pair of jeans Layla had been eyeing or even hire someone to fix the damn door! No. This money would go to paying her mom's bills, but it was fun to dream if only for a moment.

Val gave herself a pep talk in the shower. She deserved this. After years of hard work for the magazine, she had proven herself. And she'd changed, right? Ugh, Sonia was going to play hardball about time in the office, though, she could feel it.

"I will agree to all mandatory meetings," she told her washrag, "but I swear to god, if HR wants to call a meeting about office etiquette or some other bull, I will not be there."

She stopped her body scrubbing and took a moment to breathe, letting the warm water cascade down her back. Getting upset so quickly was not a good sign. "Just agree. Don't fight. Just agree. Whatever it is. You can do it." The voicemail from the nursing home echoed in her brain. She had to do it.

Val pulled on a pair of jeans that sported a few fashionable tears above the knee and a vintage Smashing Pumpkins T-shirt. She topped it off with a black sport coat and matching Vans, feeling like the epitome of cool. Professional and still in touch with the youths. Although Layla would surely call this outfit "try hard." But it was the best she could do at the moment.

• • • •

SONIA'S OFFICE WAS high-end minimalism. A wall of windows with a stunning view of the Flatirons and a perfectly polished glass top desk with not so much as a fingerprint on it. The clutter one might expect from a magazine editor sat at the back of the room. Magazine issues lay open and spread across a table. The cork board hanging above it was covered in colorful sticky notes and arranged like the layout of the magazine itself.

Val kicked her leg as she waited for Sonia. She reminded herself to smile, to breathe, to not tell anyone to fuck off.

"Hey, Val." Sonia swept into the office, decked out in a pair of khaki cargo pants and a bright, orchid-colored Patagonia jacket. With her nut-brown hair pulled back into a ponytail and a pair of Raybans perched on her head, she encapsulated Boulder fashion: ultra high-end, expensive, but make it appear like a hike will be had over lunch.

Sonia smiled at Val in the way she always did—tight-lipped, never quite reaching her eyes. "How are you?"

This was not the question a friend or casual acquaintance might ask with the expectation the answer was "fine." No, this question was loaded. It implied, "Are you mentally stable?" "Beat anybody up lately?" "Do you feel angry right now?" It was a lot.

Val reminded her facial muscles to do that thing she needed to do to become employed once more.

"I'm doing great, Sonia, thank you for asking." Her cheeks strained.

"Good. Because I loved your latest submission and would like to offer you your job back. On a trial basis, of course."

The relief that swept over her nearly knocked Val off her chair. A regular paycheck! No more freelancing! Health insurance! She could finally call the home back and agree to a payment plan and wouldn't have to do any mathematical gymnastics to keep her lights on.

Val mentally high-fived herself and let out the breath she had been holding. "That's great, Sonia. Thank you."

Sonia put a hand out to stop her. "On a trial basis, of course." As if Val hadn't heard her the first time.

"Yes, of course!" She would prove to Sonia that she deserved to be here. Show up to all staff meetings, maybe even with a smile on. At least, she'd try.

"Listen," Sonia said, a shadow falling over her face, "the board is not thrilled about my desire to have you back on staff after your little..." She waved her hand in the air as if shooing away a rotten smell. "Incident."

Never mind that the incident in question was a direct result of her getting fired in the first place, but now was not the time to bring this up.

"I'll be on my best behavior, I promise." And Val meant it. She would do whatever she had to do. Within reason.

"I know you will." Sonia's expression softened, and she reached over the desk and clasped Val's hands.

Val stiffened. What in the hell was happening? Since when did they become an office that displayed affection? Sonia's ice-cold fingers gave hers a squeeze, and Val tried to pretend this wasn't the weirdest thing that had ever happened at work.

"Your submission was so lovely and raw, at first I couldn't believe it was something you had written. But then I remembered that you were in therapy, and wow, it really sounds like it's doing wonders for you."

"Uh, yeah."

What? Val wouldn't call an inside look at the dark side of children's beauty pageants "lovely and raw." There wasn't anything lovely about it. And what did this have to do with her therapy?

Sonia finally let go of her hands and flipped open her laptop, her face changing into business mode. "When is your birthday?"

This felt like something HR would handle, but Val played along. "May."

"So you have seven months to complete your goal, but let's say six since we publish a month ahead." Sonia's face scrunched, looking up as if the plan she was formulating was written on the ceiling.

Where the hell was this conversation going?

"We obviously can't publish every letter you write, but let's say we do one a month with a writeup of how your journey is going. Readers are going to love seeing your vulnerability and grow right along with you."

Val's head spun. What was Sonia talking about? Her letters? She didn't submit her letters! She struggled to wrap her brain around what was happening, but she didn't want to show it.

Sonia cocked her head. "Does that sound okay to you?"

Val shook her head, wondering if she'd heard correctly. "Just to clarify, you want to publish my letters?"

"Yes, the challenge you set for turning forty? What did you call it?" Sonia tapped her chin and scrunched her face. "Your journey of self-improvement? Honestly, it's a great idea."

The confusion cloud in her brain snagged on a bit of that statement. *Journey of self-improvement.* Where had she heard that? Because it didn't sound like her at all. And the memory of Maddie on her living room floor gushing about the journey Val had embarked on came flooding back to her.

That conniving little shit.

"I love the idea of self-improvement. If I were to do something for my fortieth, I think it would be to complete the Ironman." Sonia looked almost wistful. Now this made so much sense.

"Let me stress again, this is on a trial basis," Sonia said, back to business again. "I'm placing my faith in you and trust that you will behave yourself in a professional manner. And, Val, you need to show up, don't miss a single deadline. I love this feature for you, but any screwups, and I have to let you go. Do you understand?"

Val could only nod. Heat rose to her cheeks, and she tried to play it off as contrition, embarrassment, instead of the volcano of fury she could suddenly become. She had to remind herself that she was getting her column back, and nothing else mattered. This was what she wanted. Sonia waved her out, and Val had to keep herself from sprinting out of the office and shouting at Maddie in the bullpen.

Maddie, the one who played cute and innocent, had betrayed her. She had gone behind her back and did the one thing Val said she didn't want to do. Her heart slammed a rhythm against her chest as if it wanted to jump out of her ribs and pound Maddie to a pulp on her behalf. Val forced her feet to take slow, measured steps to the door, reminding herself to breathe.

"Oh, and one more thing," Sonia said as Val placed her hand on the doorknob.

Val turned. "Yes?" Though could she really handle one more thing?

Sonia offered her a smile and said, "I forgive you."

What the hell? Val huffed a laugh, which Sonia must have taken for a "thank you" as she turned back to her laptop.

Val stalked over to where her old desk sat, abandoned, just as she had left it. Well, at least she wouldn't have to fight the interns for a place to work now that she was back.

Maddie stared at her laptop screen, and she typed furiously, clearly in the zone. Personal effects cluttered her desk. Framed photos, drawings from a niece she couldn't stop bragging about, stuffed animals probably from her childhood and other sentimental garbage scattered everywhere. Val slapped a hand on the only square inch of desk she could see, making Maddie jump in her seat. Good. Val's brain was unconsciously devising a revenge plan.

Startled, Maddie threw a hand to her chest and pushed her chair back from her desk. Val crossed her arms and delivered a death stare.

Maddie laughed nervously. "Val! What are you doing here?"

As if she didn't know. "Oh, I have my column back. I work here now." Val smiled, the kind of smile a psycho gives its murder victim before slashing them in half. Or so she suspected.

"Oh, my gosh, that's amazing!" Maddie reached out and grabbed Val's hand. "I'm so happy for you!"

Val twisted her face. "What did you do, Maddie?"

Maddie flung a cautious glance around the room and then motioned for Val to lean in. "I was just trying to help," she said in a low voice. "And it worked!" She was clearly pleased, her smile growing.

Val leaned in and growled, "You and me. Outside. Now."

• • • •

THE OCTOBER BREEZE bit at her face, forced Val's hands into the pocket of her jeans, and made her wish she had brought along her hoodie. Maddie exited the building behind her, her shoulders drooping ever so slightly. Val just grunted and walked in the direction of the shops along the pedestrian mall. They couldn't stay out here in this weather, but they needed to get far away from the building before Val exploded. She couldn't risk her coworkers witnessing another meltdown on her first day back. That wouldn't instill much confidence, now would it?

Maddie hugged her arms around her middle. "I left my sweater in the office. Come on." She tugged Val in the direction of the closest shop. Sweet warmth enveloped them as they pushed their way inside. Maddie certainly hadn't been interested in getting yelled at this morning because she had pulled them into the bookstore. Great.

"Good morning" came a cheerful voice from behind the counter.

"Yeah, right." The sarcasm barked out of Val unwittingly. Maddie gave Val's arm a little smack and doubled down with a stern expression, like she couldn't believe Val had said that. Didn't she know Val enough by now?

Val closed her eyes, took a breath, and gave the cashier a small smile. "Sorry."

She rubbed her bare arms to tamp down the goose bumps as the source of her annoyance led her to the back of the store. Maddie stopped at a table in the self-help section and plopped down.

"Whatever you do, please don't make a scene," Maddie whispered.

Val scowled. "I turned in an article on beauty pageants, so why did Sonia think I pitched my letters? With a sample letter and everything? I did no such thing."

"I was just trying to help." Maddie shot her those big, annoying puppy dog eyes. "She loved the idea, right?"

"Yes! But why? And what did she mean, 'I forgive you'? What did you do?" One would think that the money that would soon be deposited into her bank account would make Val feel a touch more charitable. It didn't.

Maddie shrank into herself for a moment before uncurling and sitting up straighter. It was almost as if she had taken enough of everyone's crap, and she wasn't going to allow it anymore. Good for her. But still, did she have to grow a pair right now?

"You have something there. Those letters, this journey you're on. It's inspiring, and because I knew you wouldn't do anything about it, I went ahead and pitched it to Sonia on your behalf."

"With what? Did you hack into my computer?"

At this, Maddie looked sheepish. "No. I wrote one."

Val took a deep breath. This was what she had feared. "You wrote a sample letter, pretending to be me?"

Maddie nodded, her smile faltering.

"And who, pray tell, was this letter addressed to?" Val's body nearly vibrated with aggravation, knowing full well what Maddie was about to say.

"Sonia." It came out in a whisper. Maddie's gaze fell to the table. At least she had the decency to be ashamed.

Val closed her eyes and focused on her breathing. She wasn't going to explode here in the middle of the bookstore. Maddie was her friend, and she wasn't going to yell at her.

"Let me read it," Val said, holding out her hand.

"I don't think that's—"

"Maddie, I'm as serious as climate change," Val growled. "Hand it over."

With her brows furrowed and obvious regret filling her eyes, Maddie pulled out her phone and tapped at the screen. Once she had the page pulled up, she said, "This was for your own good, remember that." Then she thrust the phone at Val.

Words sprang off the screen, and it was all Val could do to not throw the phone across the room. "As my mentor...your unwavering support..." Ugh. "Single mother...lost control...incredibly regretful for my actions."

Val dropped the phone like it was a grenade. If only, though, she wouldn't mind blowing off the face of the earth at this very moment.

"Maddie, no! This doesn't sound like me. Besides, I didn't punch Sonia in the face, what am I apologizing to her for?"

"You embarrassed her with your behavior. It was all anyone talked about for weeks."

Val pressed the heels of her hands against her eyes. "You totally crossed a line!" What had Maddie been thinking?

"I know. I'm sorry," Maddie said. "But it had to be done. You weren't going to do it yourself, and I know this job is so important to you. Now we get to work together again, and you can pay your bills."

Val sat back in her chair, not knowing what to think. She had her column back, and that was all she wanted, wasn't it? But now she had to publish her letters. Open herself up and be...vulnerable? She was still telling herself lies, how could she share the truth of her life with the general public?

And then it hit her: She didn't have to publish her letters at all. She could make them up, and no one would be the wiser. Val had always wanted to try her hand at fiction, so why not start now? It might even make it easier, hammering out sappy bullshit that readers could connect with. Val would be the only to know that it wasn't real.

Maddie teetered, visibly trying to hold on to her confidence and not crumble into a thousand apologies. And even though Val wanted to throw her into the icy waters of Boulder Creek, she took a deep breath and said, "You're right. I have my job back, and that's all that matters."

Bills would be paid, her mother wouldn't have to move. And once she got through this ridiculous assignment, she could write whatever she wanted again. Val could do this, right?

Chapter 18

"I'm so glad you were free today, hiking alone is depressing," Rupa said, flinging an arm over Val's shoulder. "It's nice to have a short break from all the gigs. I finally get to see the light of day."

"I didn't realize you lived so close to the foothills."

Located in North Boulder, Rupa's apartment butted up against a spacious park where kids could be found playing any number of sports. Val had no idea what they were playing today. Cricket? Lacrosse? Kids were running and holding sticks, and it certainly didn't look easy. Val sent a silent message of thanks to the god of Nerdy Kids that she was gifted an indoor child. Val couldn't imagine having to spend every Saturday morning on the sidelines of some sporting event, pretending to care.

Rupa spread her arms wide and let out a cheery shout. "It's so damn beautiful today!"

Clouds filled the October sky, and aside from having just entered sweater weather, there was nothing Val enjoyed more than a reprieve from the burning sun.

"And I hear congratulations are in order. I knew you'd get your job back, you've always been tenacious," Rupa said, lightly socking her in the arm.

Tenacious would be one word to describe her but maybe also stupid. Val just chuckled.

"Well, then tell me, what are you writing about now?"

"You're not going to believe me," Val said, running her hand through the tall grasses that sprang up on either side of the trail. The gentle shushing sound and soft tickle of the dried plumes set off something nostalgic in her. Maybe Val really did need to get outside more often.

"Try me," Rupa said.

"I've decided to take on a self-improvement challenge. You know, like you suggested."

"Shut up!" Rupa flung a hand out and smacked Val in the shoulder, a bit harder than Val would have liked.

"Jesus, woman." Val rubbed the point of contact, thankful for her fleece to provide a little extra padding.

"Sorry, it's just that you never listen to me. I got overly excited. So what are you doing for your challenge? It's clearly not anything remotely related to exercise, I can tell."

Val huffed out a laugh. "No, it's not. I'm writing letters. Forty of them. And Sonia really liked that idea, so that's what my column is now about."

"Wow. You, sharing your deep emotional thoughts with the entire metro area? I'm impressed."

"Don't be. It's all lies." Val waved her hand in the air as if it were no big deal. "I have my job back, so this assignment was just a means to an end, you know." A cramp teased its way into Val's side, and she slowed down. "Please don't make me talk about work anymore."

Rupa threw her hands in the air. "Fine by me."

After several tight switchbacks, the trail eased into the woods. The forest greeted them with the hint of pine in the air and the whooshing of a distant breeze. Under the tree cover, the temperature cooled a few degrees, but it was heaven. Except that it was getting harder to breathe.

"Oh, I've been meaning to ask, how's school going for Layla? Did those rumors ever stop?"

"She's a beast right now. She hardly says— Wait, how did you know about the rumors?"

Rupa shrugged. "She texts me sometimes, that's all."

"Really?"

"Of course she does, I'm her godmother."

Huh. Unmistakable jealousy rose up in Val. She made herself available to Layla all the time, and here she was, confiding in Val's best friend instead.

"Did she...did she tell you what the rumors were about? She barely talked to me about it."

"No. Kids are dicks, though, it could have been anything."

"What kinds of things does she tell you?"

Rupa laughed. "That you need to stop being so nosy."

"Very funny."

Even though this new development irked her, she decided not to push it. "Did you know that Peter bought her an iPhone, and I didn't even know about it?"

Rupa shrugged. "I'm sure her friends had iPhones in elementary school."

"This town is weird."

"And that's what I love about it," Rupa said. "Although I prefer the crunchy weird, not the uber rich weird."

"You and me both. Christ, let's slow down," Val said, holding her side. "I've got a cramp."

"We can take a break if you want, but we're super close to an amazing view."

"Okay, just a second." Val let her backpack drop to the ground, shrugged out of her fleece, and tied it around her waist. She took a big swig from her water bottle. Her lungs compressed, and she absently wondered if this was how she would die.

Rupa did the same. "Are you okay? When was the last time you exercised?"

"I don't exercise." Val bent forward, her elbows on her knees, and took a few breaths.

"Have you learned nothing? Exercise is good for you."

Val swiped her hand in the air. "Propaganda."

Rupa barked out a laugh. "Fine."

When they finally reached the overlook, Val was wheezing, and her shirt clung to her, sweat coating the skin where her backpack rested. She flung the pack off and spread her arms wide to catch the chilly breeze in her sweaty pits.

"Over here." Rupa made her way onto a large rock at the edge of the mountain. The entire city of Boulder sprawled in front of them, Denver's skyscrapers popping up in the distance. It was breathtaking. They were like giants on the mountain, the city below them merely a child's playset. A car wound its way up to the National Center for Atmospheric Research, turning this way and that up the switchbacks. And from their vantage point, all Val could picture was a giant toddler grabbing the little car, swinging it back and forth yelling, "Zoom! Zoom!"

Val plopped down with a sigh and was gratified when she heard Rupa breathing a bit harder, too. They munched on their energy bars and soaked up the solitude.

"This never gets old," Rupa said in a quiet voice as if not wanting to break the silence.

Val wordlessly agreed. She sucked in a lungful of fresh mountain air, and between the scent of the pines and the view, it was like a soul cleanse. Maybe she should do this more often.

She stretched her legs out and took one last look over the city below, wishing they could stay and not have to get back to reality. But she had an article to write.

An article that was due tomorrow.

An unfamiliar sort of panic crept into her brain. Deadlines had always been a bit arbitrary for her in the past, but she couldn't afford any screwups. Not this time.

Chapter 19

Val's fingers hovered over the keyboard, itching to type but not sure what. She needed this first article to prove to Sonia that she had it in her, well, to prove to herself that she had it in her. It needed to be inspiring and motivating. Vulnerable? Ugh, she hated that word. Evelyn used it in just about every sentence during her sessions, she didn't need to use it herself. But this was what Maddie had pitched, and this was what Sonia was expecting. She could do it, right?

She propped her feet up on the ottoman and wiggled in her chair to get comfortable, but it was no use. Her muscles ached from all the damn exercise yesterday, and her hip joints screamed at her when she sat down. After struggling to get out of bed that morning, Val had the briefest inclination to try some yoga to stretch herself out, but she instantly karate chopped that idea.

Maybe a pillow behind her back would help. A down-filled chocolate-colored square sat on the sofa, squished and lifeless, but within reaching distance. She crammed it behind her back, and the pressure on her tailbone instantly released. Christ, she was so old.

Turning her attention back to her laptop, Val commanded her fingers to type. If she could just get through this one introductory paragraph, she would deem this writing session a success.

Have you ever found yourself in a situation where you were not in control? Of your body, your actions, or anything happening around you? That's where I was just a handful of months ago, spinning out of control and completely losing it. I even beat up a guy. For those of you who know me personally, you might question how that could happen given my short stature and noodly arms, but it's true, I crushed his face. And I'm not proud of that.

She snorted. Suckers. She'd do that shit again in a heartbeat. Well, she wouldn't actually, but it was nice to know that she could. Tapping her fingers lightly over the keys, she contemplated what to say next. She needed to give a reason for her ballsy actions. One that would garner a little sympathy, maybe.

I will not make excuses for my poor behavior. What I did was terrible, and I'm truly sorry for the hurt I've caused. But we all know that outside forces can wreak havoc in our lives from time to time, causing us to make decisions we wouldn't normally make and do things we wouldn't normally do. Sadly, this was one of those times for me.

A picture of her mother curled up in a wheelchair sprang to her mind. But just as quickly, she kicked that thought to the curb. This was no longer about her but about a made-up version of her. Someone else entirely.

You see, my best friend had been sick. Gladys, my beloved golden retriever, had stopped enjoying her morning walks and refused to go to the dog park (can you even imagine?). I found out that morning that her body was riddled with tumors and that I would need to send her over the rainbow bridge. It was a punch to the gut.

Had Val lost her mind? She had no idea where she was going with this. She didn't even like dogs. What if someone she knew read this and called her out? Oh, who was she kidding, no one would read this. And even if they did, golden retrievers were saints. Val wouldn't be surprised if a reader started a GoFundMe for the medical bills of this nonexistent dog. Would that be so terrible? She did have bills to pay, after all.

Devastated and furious about losing someone I love, I lost myself in a swirling storm of emotions and took it out on the first person to get close enough. Rest assured, my therapist has assigned me to do some introspective work, to focus on gratitude and forgiveness and really hone in on the root cause of my abhorrent actions. And this is the work I would like to share with you.

Val had to hold back a retching sound at the word forgiveness. If this was the garbage she would have to write to get paid, so be it, but it didn't mean she was going to like it. At all.

She closed her laptop and packed up her things. There was only so much touchy-feely stuff she could handle in one day, and this was her limit. Besides, Sonia wouldn't be afraid to let her go if she didn't make it to the staff meeting on time.

• • • •

TWENTY MINUTES LATER, and Val was already regretting her life decisions. What had she been thinking, coming back here? Val glanced around the office and found zero people she had any connection with. Susan, who treated her cat as her most precious child and wanted everyone to know about it. Derek, who wore flip-flops year-round and made a habit of throwing his nasty feet on his desk whenever he needed to think about something. Not to mention all the other losers, freaks, and know-it-alls.

And then there was Maddie, typing furiously on the other side of her cubicle. When she glanced up and met Val's gaze over their shared wall, she smiled. Okay, maybe this wouldn't be so bad, after all. At least one person was rooting for her.

Sonia stood at the front of the room decked out in so much North Face apparel she could model for their outdoor issue.

"And you all remember Val," she said, gesturing Val's way.

A groan came from somewhere in the back of the room. What a warm welcome.

"She's going to once again spearhead the features column on a trial basis. But I think we can all agree, we're looking forward to what she has to say in the coming months."

Sonia cast a glance around the room where reluctant heads nodded and shoulders shrugged. Why had she agreed to attend staff meetings again? Couldn't this be done over email?

Val tapped her foot and stared out the window. It was bright as hell outside, as usual, the sun lighting up the Flatirons and reminding her of what a gorgeous place she lived in. The aspens had begun to turn in the last few weeks, dotting the stretch of green up the mountains in their signature gold. Maybe she should take Layla out this weekend to see the fall foliage. When was the last time they did something like that? It was all errands, appointments, school, work. Sometimes, being sucked into the tedium of parenthood and having to be an adult all the time distracted her from the beauty surrounding her every day.

Sonia cleared her throat, bringing her out of her daydream. "Val?" All eyes were on her.

"I'm sorry. What was that?" Val shifted in her seat, tucking her feet under her chair to keep them from bouncing.

"I just thought you might have something to say to the group. It's been a few months since you've been here." Sonia raised her eyebrows, a small smirk tugging at her lips. She was clearly enjoying this humiliation. What was she expecting here? An apology? Did she want Val to grovel?

Val sat up straighter and pushed down the impulse to flip them all off and march right on out of there. "Yes, thank you, Sonia. I appreciate the opportunity." She gazed around the room and did her best impression of someone who cared and said, "It's good to be back."

The room was silent but for a click of a pen. No one looked her way. She could have gotten this cold reception at home with Layla.

"I'll do my best to fill Coke—" Val recalled what Maddie had said about not everyone enjoying her sense of humor and quickly corrected herself. "Uh, Cari's shoes." Val narrowed her eyes and scanned the room. "Where is she, anyway?" It wasn't that Val wanted to seek revenge on the energetic sock puppet, per se, but she wouldn't turn down the opportunity if it presented itself.

All eyes looked up and abruptly back down. Sonia cleared her throat. "Well, it's no secret. She's in rehab."

A bark of laughter erupted out of Val; she couldn't help it. Cari should have been in rehab months ago, and Val had called it! But no one else thought this was amusing in the least, as evidenced by their judgmental stares and stony silence. Okay, fine.

Val coughed to hide her amusement and quickly mumbled, "I'm glad she's getting help," before sitting down. And she was glad. About Cari getting the help that she needed, sure. But what Val loved more than anything was being right.

Maddie turned toward Val, her eyes bulging and a *what the hell?* expression written all over her face. Val shrugged. Everyone hated her already, so what difference did it make?

When Sonia finally shut her trap, releasing them all to do their jobs, Val opened her laptop and stared at her article. Was there vulnerability here? Was she opening up enough? It was hard to tell given it was all a bunch of fiction.

• • • •

AN HOUR LATER, VAL had to keep herself from banging her head against her laptop. Like an addict in desperate need of a fix, Val was dying to spring from her seat and sprint out of the building. In her negotiations with Sonia, which really weren't negotiations at all, Val had agreed to spend more time in the office. Staff meetings were one thing, but working at this physical desk was torture. How could she concentrate with all the distractions swirling about? Clicking from a dozen keyboards, the buzz of the fluorescent light overhead, and the god awful chitchat coming from the breakroom. *No one wants to hear about your stupid cat, Susan!*

Did she really need to be here? Of course, the answer was yes, as evidenced by the bills piled on her kitchen counter, but Val found it baffling that she questioned it at all. This job had been her dream, and she had loved it. Once upon a time, anyway. When had that changed?

Her phone alarm buzzed on her desk, signaling for her to leave and pick Layla up from school. She eyed her article. Was it perfect?

Absolutely not. Good enough, though? She hit the send button and crossed her fingers.

Chapter 20

"Do you want to watch a movie with me tonight? I'll have to figure out where I can stream it and maybe get Maddie or Rupa's login. Someday, we'll have Netflix again, I swear. I just need that first paycheck." Val rambled as she shoved her laptop into her bag, gearing up for a trip to the office that would determine her fate at the magazine. How did Sonia take it? She honestly wanted to throw up.

"I won't be here." Layla picked at her cinnamon pancakes, her attention glued to her phone screen.

Val stopped what she was doing and stared at her, the queasiness turning into confusion. For a moment, she wondered if she had gotten the weekend wrong, but no. It was Val's weekend with Layla, so why didn't this feel right?

"Oh, okay. And where are you going?"

Layla shrugged, refusing to look at her. "I've got plans."

"Would you mind sharing what these plans are, please?" Val had a right to know; after all, she was the mother here.

"Why do you always want to know everything?" Layla pushed herself up from the table and grabbed her backpack off the floor.

Because Val *needed* to know everything! What would happen if she was left in the dark all the time? Nothing good, that's for sure. Val's mother hadn't known, never cared to know what Val had been up to, and look where that got her. Visions of Layla with that boy from the mall, kissing, touching. No!

"Are your plans with Dillon?" She had tried to say it casually, but it certainly came out frantic and uncool.

Layla glared at her over her shoulder. "What if they are?"

Val's head spun with reasons that would be a terrible idea. Teenagers were not capable of making smart decisions, she knew this all too well. But at least Layla had someone on her side, someone who was looking out for her. Someone she never had.

"I'm calling the doctor's office and making you an appointment."

Layla had her shoes on, ready to walk out the door, but she turned around. "What for?"

"If you're going to spend time with boys, I think it's time we put you on birth control. You know, just in case."

Layla scoffed. "I don't need that, Mom."

"It's a good idea to stay protected, honey." But it was too late, Layla was out the door without another word.

Val sighed as she picked up Layla's abandoned breakfast dishes and rinsed them in the sink. The last thing she needed greeting her at the end of the day was an army of ants marching sticky syrup all over the kitchen table.

What was she going to do with this kid? No matter how bad she wished to have control over who Layla spent her time with, rationally, Val knew she didn't. She could track her phone all she wanted but couldn't always be there to guide her in making smart choices. Smarter choices than she made at that age.

But this was one thing she could do to help. Val picked up her phone and dialed the number to Planned Parenthood.

Chapter 21

Val leaned forward in the office chair as Sonia tapped a perfectly manicured finger on her desk. With nerves on high alert, threatening to implode from the anxiety, Val couldn't help but hold her breath.

"I read through your first submission this morning and I have to say..." Sonia scrolled on her laptop screen as if she was going to read the damn thing again right in front of her.

Say what, woman?

She finally met Val's gaze. The corners of her mouth were drawn up in what might be a smile, it was hard to tell. Why couldn't she have a face that gave away something, anything? Instead, she was a brick wall.

"Yes?" Val couldn't wait anymore, the suspense was killing her. Did Sonia like it, did she hate it? Was Val destined to take a job bagging groceries or could she live to see another writing day?

Sonia sat back in her seat and steepled her fingers. "As far as apologies go, it's weak. You didn't really apologize. Instead, you shifted the blame onto your dog. Sorry for your loss, by the way, but this leads me to believe you've learned nothing."

A bowling ball dropped into Val's stomach, and her bank account wailed in agony. It hadn't worked. Of course it hadn't worked, it hadn't been her idea in the first place. She didn't want to write these stupid letters, even if they weren't true. Sonia's expression became thoughtful, and Val steeled herself to be let go once again.

"However," Sonia said in a way that made Val straighten in her seat. However? Sonia tossed that "however" like a life preserver into Val's sea of self-pity, and Val clung on to it with all her might. So much hope in one single word.

Val held her breath as Sonia continued. "You did show a vulnerability that I didn't think you were capable of. And Gladys is going to be a hit."

And then Sonia smiled. In her head, Val hoisted a fist in the air like Judd Nelson at the end of *The Breakfast Club*. After all those hours spent agonizing how to get back in here, she'd finally done it. Victory. While what she had written held only a sliver of truth, it had fooled Sonia and would no doubt fool the masses.

Before Val could congratulate herself too much, Sonia leaned forward on her desk and narrowed her eyes. "I didn't know you had a dog."

That bowling ball in her stomach rolled around. She was so close, she had to salvage this.

Val cleared her throat and said, "What can I say? Pandemic puppy."

Sonia's face relaxed, and she nodded as if this made perfect sense. Everybody got a dog during those weird years, right? Everyone except for Val, that is. But that didn't matter because Sonia had bought it.

"Well, the readers will latch on to Gladys right away. Great hook. Just dig a little deeper with your next submission." Sonia nodded and turned her attention back to her laptop, signaling the meeting was adjourned.

"Thank you." Val made a swift exit, grabbed the collar of her T-shirt, and flagged away a rising warmth in her body. That was a close one. But she did it!

She pranced down the hall, feeling like a kid who got away with stealing a bottle of gin from their parents' liquor cabinet. Bills would certainly be paid, and her nightmare of wearing a Whole Foods apron could disappear. Now she just needed to think of what to write next.

• • • •

THE DRIVE TO EVELYN'S office that afternoon had the sun careening into Val's corneas. But she didn't mind. She popped on her sunglasses, adjusted her visor, and hummed along to an old Journey song that rumbled through the speakers. Nothing would destroy her good mood today!

Steve Perry's voice cut out abruptly, replaced by the ringing of her phone over the Bluetooth. Val stabbed at the buttons on her steering wheel to ignore the call, but she must have hit the wrong one because Peter's voice boomed through her car.

"Hello? Val? I know you're there." She had been wrong, there was something that could burst her bubble. He was the last person she wanted to talk to.

"I'm here. What do you want?" she said, irritated that Peter had interrupted one of her favorite songs.

"We need to talk about Layla."

And just like that, Val's mood shifted from slightly annoyed to worried. Their interaction that morning had played over and over again in Val's mind. And although she was absolutely right about their next move, it was probably time to bring Peter in on the conversation. Which she obviously didn't want to do.

"You're right," Val said, internally groaning at the phrase she usually avoided saying.

"She's a bit of a handful these days, isn't she?"

Finally, something they could agree on. "A little more than a handful. She's obstinate, defiant, and she has plans tonight and won't tell me what they are. I don't know who she's going to be with, where, or when she's coming home. It's too much."

"It's probably debate team practice," Peter said.

"As if she's on the debate team." Val laughed to herself. She couldn't imagine her shy, quiet child doing something so ballsy.

"Well, she is. They have a big debate tomorrow after school."

What? Add that to the list of shit Val was the last to know. She made a mental note to find out more from someone other than Peter. She was constantly chewing him out for not knowing things, and here she was, in the dark.

"Listen," Peter's voice came back over the line as casual as ever. "Layla is a teenager. She's in a stage where her body is changing, and she's not always in control of her emotions and—"

"Are you mansplaining puberty to me right now?" She didn't mind the change of subject, but seriously? Like she didn't know what hormones could do to a developing girl at that age.

Peter breathed in audibly and let it out so aggravatingly slow, centering himself for his next golf swing or his next words, it was hard to tell.

"She might need some space, that's all I'm saying," he said in a calm and measured tone. "Give her a little breathing room to figure herself out."

"She's probably hanging out with a boy tonight! We need to do something before..." She didn't want to say the words out loud.

There was a knowing silence over the phone, as if they were both transported back to when they were teens. Unchaperoned on a Friday night, hot and heavy in the backseat of Peter's car.

"You think she's going to have sex before she's ready," Peter said.

"Yes!" How could she not think that? "I made her an appointment to discuss birth control options—"

"I know," Peter said, cutting her off gently. "That's why I'm calling. Layla's not there yet."

"How could you possibly know that?"

"She texted me this morning and asked me to talk you off the ledge."

Val turned a corner, and the sun shifted, blasting her eyeballs once more. She leaned to the left and stretched herself up to hide behind the visor while keeping her attention on the road.

"Talk me off the ledge?" Val's voice rose an octave. She hadn't been on the ledge! If anything, she was on one right now.

"Listen, you have to trust her." He said this with compassion, that much was clear. But it didn't make it any easier to hear. "She knows what she's doing, and honestly, she's more prepared than we ever were. More prepared than any of her friends, I'm sure."

Val gripped the steering wheel until her knuckles turned white, refusing to let herself believe that her daughter was prepared for any of it. This was not how she thought this conversation would go. Layla called Peter behind Val's back? It was like a kick to the gut. They were supposed to be a team, her and Layla.

"She's going to do that stuff when she feels ready, when she wants to, it's not up to us."

"I just don't want her dealing with any regrets," Val said.

"I know."

"No, you don't know, you weren't there!" Val snapped. No one had been there. She had been fourteen, pregnant, and absolutely alone. She would never want Layla to experience something so terrifying.

"You didn't want me there, remember? You pushed me away like you always do. Besides, Layla isn't you."

Val punched at the steering wheel buttons, finally hitting the right one to disconnect the call. And even though she didn't want to admit it, Peter was right. Layla was her own person. So why wasn't this easier?

Chapter 22

After Val's conversation with Peter, being questioned by Evelyn was like a punch to the face.

"Let me get this straight. You're getting paid to publish what essentially started as a therapy assignment?" Evelyn's voice held skepticism, something Val didn't hear from her often. She was usually void of emotion other than a façade of friendliness.

"No." Val shook her head. "Well, sort of." Telling Evelyn hadn't been on her list, but Evelyn had a habit of weaseling information out of her unwittingly. "I'm not actually going to publish the ones I write for you."

"For you," Evelyn corrected, "but go on."

"Okay, I'm not going to publish the ones I write for myself. I'm just going to write different ones, specific for outside consumption."

"Fake letters then?"

"Well, I wouldn't call them fake. I've got issues to spare, right? Let's just call these practice letters."

Evelyn looked dubious. "Let me see if I have this right. You're going to string your readers along on a fake journey of self-improvement, lying to them about what you're learning and concocting letters to fake people about something as equally made up? And you'll get paid to do this?"

Val sank a little in her seat. "When you put it like that, it doesn't sound so great. But, yeah, I guess."

Evelyn sat up straighter, if that was possible. Where does this chick get her extra vertebrae?

"Val, you're on a journey of self-discovery. I'm not a fan of you making that public. I don't think that's something anyone should do until they've been through it and have fully had time to process what they've learned."

Self-discovery, huh? All along, she thought this was just punishment for having a bad day. Or at best, learning ways to cope with her baggage. But the thought of discovering some new part of herself made her a touch queasy. What would she learn? That she was a bit of an asshole, struggling to keep it together? Not newsworthy. If there was something else for her to uncover, Val wasn't sure she wanted to find it.

"Put your thought and energy into the letters you're writing, the ones you're writing for yourself, not the magazine. Really take the time to do those well and see how you feel. Fake something if you must, but splitting your time between what's real and what's fake isn't going to do you any favors."

Evelyn obviously had a point, but Val wasn't going to let her have that. "Listen, I need to make money. I have to pay you, don't I? And I agree, I'm not ready to expose my flaws and feelings to the world, so I'll just have to make some up for now."

"If this isn't what you want to spend your time writing, can I ask, what do you want to write?"

Val shrugged. "I was an investigative journalist before all this. I wrote shit that mattered."

"And if you could write anything, you'd go back and do that?"

Val opened her mouth to say yes, but she couldn't. If she could write anything she wanted, it certainly wouldn't have been that. A vision of her teenage self and the gold notebook she used to write in flashed through her mind. She had never been happier writing than she was back then.

Val sighed. "I honestly don't know."

"So why do you still write?" And probably sensing Val's train of thought, she hastily added, "And don't say the money. We both know it doesn't pay that well."

Touché.

"I write because it's all I've ever wanted to do. Writing a story is like putting together an elaborate puzzle. Once you get those pieces to finally fit together, it just..." She trailed off, not really able to vocalize the self-satisfaction that came with telling a story. Val shrugged. "It sounds stupid, doesn't it?"

Evelyn shook her head and smiled. "It's not stupid at all. I can relate."

"Let me guess, therapy is kind of like that?" Val said.

"Yes. People are puzzles. But it's not my job to solve you. I'm just here to help you see all the pieces."

And that was exactly what Val was afraid of.

• • • •

THE NEXT DAY, VAL WALKED down the long corridor of Layla's high school, a spring in her step. A group of students in gold blazers gathered toward the end of the hall, and a mix of emotions filled her. Her little girl was growing up, and she couldn't be more proud of her for participating in something so...extroverted. Quiet as can be at home, and here she was, about to get up on a stage and argue with some schmo from another school about who knows what. If she was anything like her mother, Layla would crush it.

Layla leaned against a locker, her attention glued to a sheet of paper. She looked so studious in an official debate team uniform, her curls tamed into a ponytail.

Val sneaked up next to her and then jumped, waving her arms in the air. "Boo!"

"Oh, my god, Mom!" Layla placed a hand over her heart and glared in Val's direction. "Are you trying to kill me?"

"Oh, honey, I'm sorry!" Val reached out for Layla's shoulders to steady her, but Layla stepped back.

"What are you doing here?" she hissed. Her eyes narrowed, and her gaze flit down the hall like she was looking for someone. Anyone but Val, apparently.

"Why didn't you tell me you were on the debate team? I would have loved to practice with you—"

"Exactly why I didn't tell you. Look, parents don't sit in the audience and watch debate, this isn't a basketball game."

"I know, honey, but I really wanted to come see you."

"But I don't want you to be here. You'll just make me nervous. Please, can you just go?"

"I'll just sit in the back. You won't even see me."

Layla pleaded with her eyes as other kids made their way past them into the auditorium, all dressed for success in their matching outfits. A couple of girls glanced their way and giggled. Val's heart sank. All she wanted was to get a glimpse into Layla's life and make a connection with her, but not if it meant humiliation.

Val held up her hands and took a step back. "Okay, okay, I'll go. Just...you know, good luck. Break a leg, or whatever the good luck equivalent is for debate."

Layla's tight smile and quick nod was the closest to a "thank you" as Val would get.

Val sighed, shoving her hands into the pockets of her jeans. Maybe this was for the best. She had a deadline to make, so she might as well get cracking.

Val woke up early the next day to beat the Saturday morning shoppers to the most pretentious, overly priced food market around: Whole Foods. Not for regular groceries, of course, she couldn't afford that. This shopping trip was a treat.

It was high time she celebrated something good in her life. Sonia liked her article enough to secure her a spot on the payroll, and Layla had come home after debate last night saying that Dillon had been grounded, which foiled all her weekend plans.

Layla would be home with her. All weekend! Cause to celebrate, indeed! And tonight, she was going to surprise Layla with the fanciest charcuterie board she had ever seen. Oh, who was she kidding, Layla spent time with kids who probably ate fancy charcuterie for an after-school snack. It didn't matter, this was what Val wanted. Artisanal cheese, small batch crackers, expensive olives, and a bottle of something red and smooth. She wanted this day to end on a high note.

Val picked up the green shopping basket and headed to the cheese aisle. She gathered the most pretentious flavors she could find: lavender honey goat cheese and a vegan white truffle cheddar for Layla, and dropped them into her basket.

Vegan cheese would certainly earn her some parental points. Val was feeling quite smug at her choices. Things were finally turning around for her, and she couldn't be happier. Riding this unusual high, she was barely aware of her surroundings, paying no mind to the price tags and ignoring the very hairy gentleman walking around with no shoes on.

She turned on her heel to find the crackers, colliding with the person behind her with a smack. Both of their shopping baskets crashed to the ground, vegetables and cheese cartwheeling across the floor.

"Oh, for fuck's sake," Val mumbled as she put her cheese back, reaching for the potatoes that had escaped from the other shopper's basket. Why couldn't people watch where they were going?

"I'm sorry."

Val's chest strummed at the sound of the voice. Light, airy, angelic. Familiar.

Val stood and handed the rogue potatoes over to the adorable bartender, the one she never called.

"Sorry," Gina said again, a small smile on her face. Her hair had been pulled up in a messy bun. The oversized sweater she wore looked soft and cozy, and for a moment, Val wanted to wrap her arms around Gina, just to find out if it was.

"No, that's my fault." Val ducked her head and stepped to the side to get out of there before Gina recognized her, but her knee caught the corner of a display stand, and she nearly fell over in pain. But she managed to catch herself, cursing this unfamiliar awkwardness she was currently experiencing.

"Oh, you're Rupa's friend, right?" Gina said.

Val popped up from behind the display and smiled as if nothing had happened. As if she hadn't jabbed a piece of metal right into a nerve and didn't want to crumple onto the floor.

She absently snatched a product from the display in front of her, as if to say, *Don't mind me, I'm just shopping.* Her brain did not fully process what it was until she had turned back to Gina, a long tube of summer sausage in her hand. She dropped it into her basket, her cheeks burning.

"Hmm? Oh, yeah. Val," she said, pointing to herself. *Oh, god, someone kill me now.*

"Right." Gina's smile faltered just a little, probably remembering how she forked over her phone number and received nothing but radio silence.

Val longed to say something. Anything. Apologize for not calling? Ask her out, maybe? She might still be a mess, but she was at least an employed mess.

But no words came.

"She's playing at The Whale again tonight," Gina continued. "Are you going to be there?"

"Oh, no. I've got a date tonight," Val said without thinking.

Gina's eyebrows furrowed. "Oh, okay."

"No! Not like that kind of date." The words rushed out of her like she was suddenly a teenager with a massive crush and zero idea how to handle it. "My daughter. A date with my daughter and..." Val gestured down to her basket with the massive roll of meat sticking out the top, the word sausage flying up to her lips. "Um, charcuterie," she finally managed to say.

It would have been a great time for the ground to open up and swallow her whole.

An endearing smirk tugged at Gina's lips, and Val's heart thumped against her ribs. She needed to get out of there before she made herself out to be more of an idiot than she actually was.

"I've gotta go." Val gestured toward the checkout.

Gina cocked her head, an amused look on her face. "Okay."

Val made a beeline to the front of the store, abandoning her dreams of olives and crackers, but she managed to swipe up a bottle of wine from an end cap before making it to the registers. She would at least need that.

Chapter 23

Val stuffed her hands into the pocket of her hoodie as she made her way to meet Maddie at The Greasy Spoon the following Monday. She lifted her chin toward the sky, the sun's warm blaze penetrating the cool October air. Boulder in the fall brought out the best in her. The best attitude, her willingness to get outside and exercise, even a strange desire to hug people. Fall was a bizarre time in her life.

Layla had probably sensed this because she had been busy all weekend avoiding Val, coming out of her room only for snacks. When Val had asked how the debate went, she shrugged and said it was fine. Val had even put on a slasher movie in hopes of enticing her from her cave, but it hadn't worked. Instead, Val's eyeballs had been subjected to gore she'd rather never witness again.

"I knew Sonia would like it," Maddie said as they sidled up to their booth.

"Okay, yes," Val admitted, "you were right. She loved it."

Maddie clapped her hands together and squealed. "Yay!"

"Just take the win. No need to be so freaking happy about it."

"Isn't it nice to be back in the office?"

"God, no. Those people suck. Did you see the looks they gave me at the staff meeting last week? Like Sonia let a disease into the building."

"Of course they don't like you. You treated them like dirt, why should they? You know, it wouldn't hurt for you to make amends."

Val curled her lip. "I'll just stay out of the office as much as humanly possible."

"You two again, huh?" Barb hulked over to them, a hand on her hip. The dark shadows under her eyes were more pronounced than usual, and her droopy breasts hung so low they almost rested on the apron cinched around her waist. Like they had given up on life.

She pulled the pencil from behind her ear. "What can I get you?"

"Barb." Val oozed sugary sweetness, this time some of it genuine. "I'll take the largest stack of pancakes you've got and a coffee. This is a celebratory breakfast!"

"If you think I'm going to ask what you're celebrating, I'm not," Barb said without looking away from her order pad.

"Oh, Barb," Maddie said, her tone soft and full of concern. "What's going on today, are you all right?"

Val's instinct was to laugh because this was the same Barb she'd known for the better part of this year. Hard, surly, an absolute grouch. But she held it back when she noticed the genuine concern in Maddie's eyes.

To Val's shock and horror, Barb swiped at her face. "It's nothing. I'm fine." But her voice cracked.

Maddie scooted farther in the booth and patted the seat next to her. "Oh, sit down, you're clearly not fine."

Barb sighed, gave the room a once-over, and dropped into the booth. Maddie reached up and placed a hand on her shoulder.

"Want to talk about it?" Maddie asked.

With a shaky voice, Barb said, "Yesterday I found out that I'm a grandma."

"Oh, wow, Barb! That's so exciting!" Maddie clapped.

"Congratulations," Val said. She crossed her fingers that she was at the very least a decade away from such news.

Barb's shoulders slumped. "You don't understand. My daughter never told me. I had to find out from someone else. The baby is a month old."

A dull ache settled in Val's stomach. She and Maddie exchanged looks. Maddie's eyebrows raised as if expecting Val to jump in at any moment. Like she had any idea what to do here. Val shrugged.

Maddie relented and took the wheel again. "What happened?"

"I thought her boyfriend was a deadbeat. I told her that she could do better. Instead, she married the guy and hasn't talked to me since.

old."

But I thought that would change when she had a family of her own."
Barb choked back a sob.

Maddie's hand rubbed slow circles on Barb's back, but her eyes pleaded with Val to do something. Say something. Val couldn't help but think of her own mother. Her chest squeezed.

"Barb, I'm so sorry." That was it? The best she could do?

"That's awful, Barb. Maybe you should call her," Maddie said.

"I don't know," Val said, because she never knew when to keep her trap shut. "My guess is that if she wanted you in her life, she'd let you know."

Maddie and Barb stared at Val, eyes wide. What? Someone needed to stand up for the daughters of the world with shitty mothers. But with the usually stoic Barb on the verge of sobs, Val could now see this wasn't the time or place for such advocacy.

"Oh, I just mean—" The buzz of her phone saved her from putting her foot in it even further. The nursing home number flashed on her screen, and she instinctively dismissed the call. She didn't want to talk about payment plans or how she hadn't been to see her mom in weeks.

Barb waved a hand in the air and pushed herself up from the booth. "I should get back to work." She glanced down at her order pad and back at Maddie. "What do you want, hon?"

Maddie placed her order, and they waited until Barb was well out of earshot to say another word.

"Holy smokes, that's awful." Maddie placed her hand over her heart. "Can you even imagine?"

Val shrugged. "Yeah. She could have been a terrible mom, we don't know."

Maddie's mouth fell open. "That's an awful thing to say! And even if she wasn't the best, doesn't everyone deserve a second chance?"

Val picked at the napkin in front of her, tearing off little sections and making a pile of napkin confetti. "This is supposed to be a celebratory breakfast. Can we talk about something other than Barb's drama?"

Maddie put her arms on the table, giving Val her full attention. "Fine. Let's talk about your article. It was so moving!"

"Really?" She couldn't keep the skepticism out of her voice; certainly Maddie would be the one to see through it all.

Maddie reached her arms across the table and clasped Val's hands. "Really." Her eyes were soft and caring. "I'm so proud of you."

Val snatched her hands away. "Why?"

Clearly wounded, Maddie said, "For taking responsibility for your actions. That's personal growth!"

"Ugh." Val slumped lower in her seat. There had been no personal growth as far as she was concerned. Maybe even a bit of a backslide, if she were completely honest with herself.

"Hey, you should be proud," Maddie continued. "This was your goal, wasn't it?"

"Well, yeah." Val tamped down the guilt that poked its little head into her gut.

Maddie had lied to get her the job back, but would she understand if she knew Val was also being deceitful? *Fake it till you make it.* Wasn't that the saying? Couldn't that be what she was doing? Faking her way through uncomfortable feelings until she felt ready to tackle her own?

"I'm just sorry I didn't know what was going on with you," Maddie said, her face drawn into a worried expression. "You never talk about stuff. Not like that, anyway."

Val waved her hand in the air to indicate how insignificant it all was. Maddie would probably freak if she actually knew what was going on. Or at the very least, offer to help in some way, or worse, bring over a casserole.

Barb lumbered over with their coffees. The fact that she placed Maddie's directly in front of her ever so gently and practically dropped

Val's out of her reach, hot liquid puddling around the mug, did not go unnoticed.

"I don't like to share personal information, that's all," Val said. "Anyway, it's not like it's a big deal. I'm a disembodied voice on a page, no one really cares about my life."

Maddie cocked her head and put a hand to her chest. "But I care about you! I care about what you're going through and am so proud of how far you've come as a person."

"And here I thought you liked me just the way I am." Val brought the steaming mug to her lips and blew on the brown sludge inside.

"You sound like a Bridget Jones movie," Maddie said.

Desperate for a change of subject, Val raised her coffee mug in the air. "To my new/old job!"

Maddie smiled, and they clinked glasses. "And maybe to love?"

Val scrunched her nose and dumped a sugar packet into her coffee. Not this again.

"You haven't asked her out yet? Val!"

"Hey, if you're so interested, you should call her. I'm sure I still have her number in here somewhere." Val gestured to her purse. Although she would never tell Maddie this, Val had almost called Gina this weekend. She felt this need to apologize for being a complete weirdo at the grocery store. But every time she pulled up Gina's contact, she chickened out.

Sensing Val's desperate need for a change of subject, Maddie cleared her throat. "So any Halloween plans?"

"Sitting at home and answering the door for trick-or-treaters, I guess." Val shrugged. If it were up to her, Layla would be at home, all dressed up and answering the door for her. Fat chance.

"Is Layla trick-or-treating, or is she too old for that?"

"Oh, if she's home, she'll probably lock herself in her room and refuse to talk to me." Val took a sip of coffee. "Like she does every night."

"Yeah, of course she does. Weren't you like this with your mom?"

Val's heart squeezed. "No, I wasn't."

In fact, Val had been so desperate for her mother's attention that she would go out of her way to sleep in the living room, hoping to catch her mom coming home late from a night on the town. Hoping to see her eyes light up at the sight of her, hoping to put a smile on her mother's face, like she did when she was little.

And even when her mother brushed her off, came home drunk or not at all, Val still craved her affection. Until one day, when it all stopped. When Val had needed her mother more than anything, and she hadn't been there.

Her phone buzzed with a new text, jolting her out of her thoughts.

Peter: *Why aren't you answering your phone? Your mother needs you.*

Chapter 24

Val spent an hour at the nursing home, rubbing her mother's back, holding her hand, and doing her best to answer questions about little Valerie, and her emotional cup had crumbled into dust. Her mother was still stuck on some idea that she harbored a gift that she desperately wanted to give her. Val wanted to find it if only to make her shut up.

Finally back at home, she took a sip of water and stared at her laptop screen. With feet propped up on the ottoman and a pillow squished behind her back, she should be well into her second article by now. Instead, the stark white page burned her eyes, and the cursor blinked mockingly.

Sonia's words drifted back to her. Dig a little deeper. Into what? Her actual feelings? If there were any feelings left, the readers would absolutely delight in that shitshow, but Val didn't have a shred of emotion in her. But even so, she had to come up with something.

A cool breeze blew in through her open window, rustling the curtain and sending a ripple of goose bumps down her arm. Val pulled the fleece blanket around her legs and threw the hood of her sweatshirt over her head but made no move to close the window. Maybe the cold air would spark some creativity in her. It wouldn't hurt to try.

She closed her eyes and took a fortifying breath. A bird twittered from the tree in her front yard, and somewhere a dog barked. And that was when it hit her. Gladys.

Based on the comment section from her first article, the readers had latched on to Gladys, sharing their condolences and even demanding photos. Val could certainly dig up a stock photo somewhere, but she would do them one better. Her next letter would be addressed to Gladys. A heartfelt, tearful expression of gratitude for her unconditional love and companionship. For making Val a kinder, more caring person. Honestly, if dogs could make someone kinder and more compassionate, maybe Val should look into that.

Nah.

One hour and a sappy document later, Val was even more wrung out than before. She had conjured a story about a woman who happened upon an abandoned puppy while out hiking a mountain trail. She brought the dog home, nursed it back to health, thinking about how she saved the pup from certain death. Only to realize that it was indeed the dog who saved her from a life of loneliness. After all the emotional back and forth, she was ready for a drink. But it was barely noon on a Tuesday. Now what?

As if the universe heard that question and wanted to answer in the worst way possible, Val's phone rang. She picked it up and checked the caller ID. Layla's school. Parental worry kicked in, and Val rushed to answer.

"Hello? This is Val."

"Hi, Val. I'm calling from Boulder High School about your daughter, Layla."

"Is she okay?"

The pause on the other end of the line made Val's heart leap.

"That's what we were wondering."

What? Shouldn't they know?

"Layla didn't show up for class this morning, and neither you nor her father marked her out as being absent today. We were calling to make sure she was all right."

Val's stomach plummeted. If she had eaten breakfast this morning, it would have surely resurfaced.

"Um, okay. Thanks for calling, we'll find her." Val hung up the phone and pulled up the tracking app. When Layla's location flashed up along Pearl Street Mall, Val couldn't help but become curious.

• • • •

VAL KEPT THE TRACKING app up on her phone as she walked along the pedestrian mall, Layla's location never changing. She stopped right outside of the Boulder Bookstore, affection for Layla blooming in her chest. Had Layla suddenly developed a love for books?

While Val had been the child to read at every spare moment, Layla avoided books as much as possible. She'd read her textbooks if she had to, but that was it. Had that changed? Could Val even get mad at her for skipping school now that she was here? If Val had been one to skip school, this would have been where she ended up, too.

She checked her phone one last time and pushed the door open. The combination of freshly printed paper and earthy incense lingered in the entry, and it was lovely, transporting her to her days as a writer for the school newspaper. One of the boys on staff had gone through a patchouli phase, and Val wasn't ashamed to admit that while the other girls drooled over the CK1-wearing jocks, it was the patchouli that lit her fire. It was no wonder she ended up with a hippie like Peter. Val inhaled deeply and pushed Peter out of her mind.

The multilevel bookstore had stairs running every which way. To get to some sections, you needed to go upstairs and then back down a different set of stairs, and Val didn't come here often enough to know where anything was.

"Can I help you find something?" A woman wearing a name tag leaned over the counter and offered Val a smile.

Where should she begin? She had no idea what Layla was even doing here.

"Um, where's your young adult section?" She had to start somewhere.

"Upstairs in the ballroom."

Val nodded her thanks. At the top of the stairs, Val scanned the ballroom, which had served as an actual ballroom once upon a time. People milled about the stacks, every available space covered in shelves, carts, and tables of books. She imagined old-timey couples waltzing their way through the stacks, stealing kisses behind the romance section.

A giggle from across the room caught Val's attention. And sure enough, at a table in the far corner sat Layla and...Dillon?

With Layla's back toward her, Val had the element of surprise in her favor. She crept up behind Layla, directing her attention to the selection of books against the wall. Far enough away to not be recognized by Dillon, but close enough to hear snippets of their conversation.

"It's going to be okay," Layla said. "We've got each other, right?"

They've got each other? What the hell did that mean? It sounded an awful lot like a conversation Val and Peter had once upon a time. A gut-wrenching conversation that started with "I'm pregnant." Val pulled a book off the shelf and, as inconspicuous as she could, turned toward their table, the book shielding her face.

She peeked over the pages, and to her horror, Layla and Dillon's hands sat intertwined in the middle of the table. Without meaning to, Val snapped the book shut, the noise echoing across the ballroom, causing a stop to all conversation.

Layla spun around, and her eyes bulged. "Mom?" she hissed. "What are you doing here?"

Great, here she was again, being embarrassing as hell. And then Val remembered that she should be the upset one.

Val crossed her arms over her chest. "Is this where they're holding class today?"

Layla rolled her eyes and slumped in her seat.

"Come on." Val motioned for Layla to get up. "I'm taking you back to school. Would you like a ride, Dillon?" She said his name like it left a bad taste in her mouth.

He shook his head, his gaze never leaving the table. At least he had the decency to appear ashamed.

Val hooked Layla's elbow and led her out of the bookstore. Layla tried to wrench away as soon as they made it outside, but Val hung on tight until they reached the car.

"What the hell, Mom?"

"Get in."

Val pulled open the car door and all but shoved Layla inside. She slammed it and leaned on it for a moment, catching her breath.

She's just a kid, and kids do stupid things.

As soon as she felt calm enough, she slid into the driver's seat and locked the doors just in case Layla tried to escape.

"I got a call from school, and they wanted to make sure you were okay. Which was weird because that's where you're supposed to be right now." Val leaned on the steering wheel, her face turned to Layla, trying to catch her eye, but Layla stared out the window. "You know what happens when you skip school, don't you?"

"I was taking a mental health day."

Val ignored her. "Your parents get into trouble. Did you know that? Truancy is a real issue, and if the state believes we aren't sending you to school, if they think we're not providing you with access to education, we could go to jail."

Maybe that would get her attention.

"Good, you deserve it." Those words hit her like a brick.

"Listen, Layla. I'm taking you to school right now, and we'll continue this conversation later, but just so you know, you're very much grounded." Val put the car in drive and groaned. "Now I have to call your dad."

At that, Layla's head whipped around to finally face her. "No, you don't have to call Dad! I'm sorry, it won't happen again, I swear! Just please don't call Dad."

This was rich. Val could be the mean parent, the one who didn't have any fun, the one who made her clean the bathroom and do her homework. And Layla was fine with that. But god forbid the nice one, the fun parent have to get mad and do any sort of discipline. Peter had always gotten off easy when it came to discipline. He could only be bothered to refer all matters to Val.

"Ask your mother." "What does your mother say about that?" He could never make any sort of parental decision, and it left Val to always be the bad guy.

"I have to call him, he's your dad. He can take you to all the sporting events, give you tickets to concerts, and buy you a freaking iPhone, but he's not going to get out of this one." Val heaved an involuntary sigh.

Sometimes, she wondered if parenting would be easier on her own.

• • • •

"YOU CAN'T JUST TAKE a mental health day and cut class." Peter sat on the edge of the sofa and raked a hand through his hair. It was weird having him back in the house. They used to curl up every Friday on that very sofa and watch movies as a family. And here they were, back together again, but the vibe was entirely different.

"Why not? Mom lets me take them all the time." Peter swiveled his head to Val.

"All the time, my ass. I let her take one." Though she was regretting that now.

Peter turned his attention back to Layla. "It doesn't matter, you skipped school. You can't do that, sweetie. We're going to need your phone."

"What?" Layla jumped up from where she had burrowed into the chair, finally feeling some heat. "But I need it!"

Val held out her hand. "You'll find a way to manage, I'm sure. We grew up without phones."

"Oh, my god, you guys are ancient!" Layla smacked her phone into Val's palm and slumped back into the chair.

"You'll have to earn our trust to get that back," Peter said.

Confiscating her phone had been Peter's idea, and while it stood to reason this would whip her into shape, Val wasn't so sure.

"And you're grounded for a month," she added.

"What?" Peter and Layla said in unison.

Peter leaned in toward Val and lowered his voice. "Don't you think that's a bit much?"

"No, I don't."

Having Layla right under her nose for a few weeks would mean that she could not only keep an eye on her, but they could hang out again. Val missed snuggling with Layla in front of the TV, playing board games, and snacking on junk food late into the night. Maybe this was her chance to get a little bit of that back. Besides, if she was home with Val, then she wasn't out doing god knows what with Dillon.

"Mom, that's so unfair!" Layla stormed out of the room, the slam of her bedroom door echoing down the hall.

"Well, I think our job here is done," Val said, heading to her bedroom, Layla's phone in hand. All she needed to do was find a good hiding spot for it, somewhere Layla wouldn't look.

"Val, I'm not sure this is the right thing." Peter stood in the doorway, his arms crossed.

Val held up the phone. "I'm not giving this back to her—"

"I'm talking about the grounding. Don't you think a month is a tad extreme?"

Val fished out her step stool and unfolded it. "You didn't see her with that boy. I did. Something is going on between them, I just know it."

She pushed around some boxes on the top shelf of her closet. It was up here somewhere, the box where she kept Layla's Christmas presents. In a plain old regular box shoved behind other plain old regular boxes. Layla had yet to find them, so it felt logical to throw the phone in there for safe keeping.

A long ocean's breath sigh came from behind her before Peter said, "Here, let me help."

Peter reached his ridiculously long arms and grabbed the one she'd been searching for. She didn't need his help, she would have found it eventually.

"Thanks." After tucking the phone into the box, she closed it back up and gave it a push to the back of her closet.

"She's going to revolt," he said as she leaned the step stool against the wall.

Val dusted off her hands and patted Peter on the chest. "This is for the best, trust me."

Chapter 25

"And how did you react to her behavior?" Evelyn sat primly perched on the edge of her white chair, her back as straight as ever. Her hair was slicked back in a bun so tight, it visibly pulled on her face. While that might cause an everlasting migraine, it could be an easy face-lift trick, right? Val contemplated trying that at home to see how that might affect her droopy eyes.

Turns out, telling Evelyn about Layla skipping school had been harder than telling Peter. It was silly, but she didn't want Evelyn to think she was a bad parent. Every parent's secret fear was to be judged. Think of Val as an asshole or a shitty person, sure, but a bad parent? No one wanted that.

"I wanted to yell at her. Hell, maybe slap her across the face, but I didn't. I was calm. Calmer than I thought I could be."

Evelyn nodded, a slight smile on her face. "You felt your feelings but kept your reaction to them in check. Nice work."

Wait, could Evelyn actually be proud of her?

Val smiled. "We've grounded her for a month!" she said, triumphant.

Evelyn's brows drew together. "Was this what you and Peter decided together?"

"Well, I had to talk him into it."

"Or did you bully him into it?"

Evelyn's question took her aback. "What do you mean?"

"I know that you and Peter don't always have the best relationship. You've said before that he doesn't handle the tough parenting issues. Is that because he doesn't want to or because you won't let him?" Evelyn sat back in her chair and crossed her legs, like she had just scored a point, and the ball was now in Val's court. Val didn't like where this was going. She wasn't a bully. Sure, she and Peter exchanged words, they always did. But it wasn't like she was the only one tossing around those daggers.

"He just wanted to take away her phone for a while, but that wasn't going to solve the issue. Layla clearly needs more supervision. She hasn't gotten what she's needed since the divorce. It's obvious she needs one of us around more often."

"Is that what she told you?"

"Ha! She's fourteen! That girl barely tells me anything." Other than all the things Val did wrong.

"She's fourteen," Evelyn countered. "Do you think it's the best time to isolate her from her friends?"

Who the hell did this woman think she was, judging Val's parenting style? Where did she get off?

"She's my daughter, I think I know what's best for her."

"Like your mother knew what was best for you?"

So this was what it felt like to be socked in the face with words. Goddamn! No, her mom didn't know what was best for her at all. But Val was nothing like her mother. Her mother had been unloving, uncaring, and never there.

"I don't have to sit here and take this." Val rose from her seat and grabbed her purse from the floor.

"The court says otherwise."

With as much force as she could, Val slammed the door behind her.

Chapter 26

A week later, Val sat in Sonia's office, waiting for feedback on her most recent article.

"Readership is up, Val. They love it." Sonia sat with her hands clasped on her pristine desk, the delicate skeletons hanging from her ears the only nod to the holiday in her entire office. "Now I know they love to hear about your dog, but this column is supposed to be about you. So maybe a little less Gladys next time." She dismissed Val with a wave of her hand.

Right. She couldn't keep throwing the dead pet card, but what did that mean? That she would have to write something meaningful? True? Shit.

"Oh, and, Val?"

Val stopped in the doorway and turned back to her.

Sonia studied her for a moment before smiling. Not her usual thin line that bordered on a grimace, but an actual smile. "Nice work," she said with a nod before turning back to her laptop.

When had Sonia praised her work before? Not that Val could remember. It was always reminders about deadlines, admonitions when she didn't show up on time. Never praise.

In place of the lift in spirit or wave of pride she should experience at those words, guilt settled in her chest, dumping a bag of marbles into her stomach. How long could she keep this up?

She walked back to her desk in a bit of a daze. What was she going to do now? Maddie's cubicle caught her eye with its loud, spooky kitsch and string of flashing orange lights. She was hunched over, attention on her screen, typing away. If only Val had that energy, that focus. If only Val was writing something she wanted to write.

Val slumped down in her chair and opened her laptop. If she could write anything in the world, what would it be? Before she had time to think about it, someone tapped her shoulder.

"Zzzzzt," Maddie said, smiling down at her.

"What?" Val said, confused.

Maddie pointed to herself, her short hair standing on end, socks and dryer sheets affixed to her blue shirt. "I'm electricity."

Oh. "Yeah, sure, whatever," Val said, dismissing her with a swat of her hand. Dressing up for Halloween as an adult was fine in Val's book, but at the office? Come on, who'll take you seriously then?

"Want to get some breakfast?" Maddie asked, all annoying pep and cheer.

"Not today, high voltage. I've got work to do."

Chapter 27

Val tapped her knuckles on Layla's door, undeterred by a new piece of construction paper taped over a section of stickers. The very detailed drawing of a hand curled into a fist with the middle finger on full display had appeared on the first day of Layla's grounding. Val pretended that it wasn't directed at her.

She swung her black cape over her shoulders and adjusted her witch hat. "It's almost time for trick-or-treaters," she called through the door. "Are you dressing up? I have some extra witch stuff if you want to be twinsies."

That would surely garner a deep groan or a "god, Mom, you're so cringe." Instead, radio silence.

Val tried a new tactic. "How about we watch one of your horror movies tonight? I know it's not Friday, but it feels like a good night for something spooky." Val kept her voice even; she didn't want to betray her neediness. The only time she got a good glimpse of Layla the last few days was when she would emerge for snacks and promptly head back to her room. Being rejected by your own flesh and blood sucked.

Still no response. Val pressed her ear to the door but struggled to hear anything. She checked her watch. Layla had been home from school for almost three hours now, and Val hadn't seen or heard from her since she walked through the front door. A niggle of worry wormed through her brain. What if Layla wasn't in there, or worse, what if she had hurt herself? This was not a possibility that Val had explored, but teenagers were so unpredictable. Their feelings so volatile, anything could happen.

Val pounded on the door this time with a sense of urgency. "Layla, I need you to come out right now. I need to know you're safe." If anything, Layla would hear the panic in her voice and assure her that she was fine. But still nothing. Val jiggled the handle, but it was locked.

She contemplated her next move. Bust down the door? Jimmy the lock somehow? Call Peter? God, anything but that.

She took a moment to breathe and clear her head. And then she remembered. As a toddler, Layla would accidentally lock herself in the bathroom, but because it was an old house, the locks were very forgiving. Val stuck a fingernail into the lock and tried to turn it, but no luck.

"Layla, I have to come in," she called, running into the bathroom for a hair clip. "It would be easier if you could just unlock the door for me and come out."

Clip in hand, Val raced to the door, and after a moment of fiddling, the lock gave way. She barreled inside the room to find it dizzyingly cluttered but no sign of Layla.

"Layla? Seriously, where are you?" Val tossed the blankets around her bed, hoping to find a human-sized lump. Nothing. She continued her search under the bed and in the closet, but there was no sign of life. And that was when the curtain fluttered. A nearly imperceptible wave but enough to pull Val's attention.

She crossed the room, her heart pounding.

A cool breeze drifted inside from the base of the window. Val pushed the window up, and just as she had feared, the screen was gone.

• • • •

DUSK HAD DESCENDED by the time Val barreled out the front door. She weaved her way through a parade of creepy creatures and princesses with glow stick necklaces, with no idea where she was going. Where did Dillon live? Who was that girl Layla sometimes talked about? Violet? Iris? She was a goddamn flower, but which one? Christ! Why couldn't she come up with a single one of Layla's friends? Her heart thundered in her chest, and it was all she could do to keep the tears at bay.

"Layla!" Val searched every figure on the sidewalk, hoping to find her somewhere. She crossed the street and, in desperation, stopped the first grownup she could find.

"Have you seen a teenager out here? She's a bit taller than me, blue streak in her hair?"

The stranger shook their head, and Val's panic rose.

Val pulled out her phone and scrolled to Rupa's number. On a big night like Halloween, she would surely be at a gig, but Val was desperate.

Rupa answered on the first ring. "Hey, did you decide to get out of your sweats and come out tonight?"

Val could barely hear her over the noise in the background. She ignored Rupa's question. "Have you heard from Layla?"

"Not today, why? What's wrong?"

"She ran away. I have no idea where she is."

There was some rustling in the background before Rupa's voice came back over the line, crystal clear this time. "Do you want me to come and help you find her? I can go back in and tell the guys it'll just be instrumentals tonight."

"No, I don't even know where to start looking. Are you sure she didn't tell you anything?"

"No, I swear." There was a beat of silence, and Val's heart sank. "Have you called Peter?"

Val raked a hand down her face. "Not yet."

"You need to call him right now. And seriously, I will drop everything, you just say the word, okay?"

Rupa was right, she had to call Peter even if it was the last thing she wanted to do. He might even be able to help.

Val ran up the steps into the house to grab her purse and keys. She'd call Peter and get in the car. To go where, she wasn't sure.

"Hey, Val, are you guys watching a spooky movie tonight?" Peter's voice was calm and easy when he answered, as if the thought of talking to Val didn't bother him one bit. She wanted to hate that about him, but right now, his compassionate tone made her eyes well up with tears.

"She ran away!"

"I don't think I know that one. Is that a horror movie?"

"Peter! This isn't a movie! Layla has run away!" Val couldn't keep the panic out of her voice if she tried. Where was she? Who was she with? What was she doing? Images of her being kidnapped and forced to do unspeakable things flooded her mind.

"Are you sure?"

"Of course I'm sure! She isn't here. She must have jumped out the window, the screen was gone."

"Where are you right now?" His voice took on a more commanding tone.

"Getting in my car. I'm going to...I'm going..." She had really hoped that something would have come to her by now.

"Just sit tight for a second. Let me check the app, try to track her phone."

"She doesn't have her phone! I took it away, remember?" Who knew how long she'd been gone? She could be anywhere by now. How were they going to find her?

"Okay, wait," Peter said. She could imagine him pacing the room and rubbing his chin. His go-to move when working out a problem at the office. "This is what we're going to do."

Val sat frozen in the front seat of her car, listening to Peter dole out instructions. Normally, this was the behavior she couldn't stand, but being a frazzled mess, she needed someone else in control right now. Even if it had to be Peter.

"Go back inside. Find her phone and start calling her contacts. Someone will know where she is. I'm heading your way right now."

"But—"

"Val, go back inside. I'll call Rupa, maybe she's heard from her."

"I called her already, she's playing tonight. She hasn't heard from Layla."

"Do you have a friend that can come and be with you?"

Rupa would be here in an instant if Val asked her to, but she wasn't her only option, was she?

"Maddie."

"Good, call Maddie first. I'm on my way, okay?"

Val swallowed around the lump in her throat, not trusting her voice.

"Okay, Val?"

She nodded and squeaked out a "yeah" before hanging up the phone and sobbing into her steering wheel.

Chapter 28

After hanging up with Maddie, Val rushed back inside the house and hurried to her bedroom. She dug out the step stool and raced to her bedroom closet. The box full of Christmas gifts that Val hadn't wanted Layla to find was shoved as far back on the top shelf as Val could get it. Standing on tippy toes, she strained to reach it but kept pushing the box farther away instead. She cursed her T-rex arms and grabbed an empty coat hanger. Using it as an arm extension, she managed to pull the box closer until finally she was able to grab it.

Val tugged the corners of the box open and sifted through the contents. The set of colored pencils, drawing paper, and funky Christmas socks she picked up on sale last year were all still there, waiting to be wrapped up and set under the tree. But the phone was missing. Val's heart slammed itself against her ribcage. She dumped the contents onto the bed just to be sure. But the phone was gone.

"Fuuuck!" She didn't know how else to get a hold of Layla's friends. What were they going to do now?

"Val?" Maddie's voice called from the living room.

"She stole her phone." Val growled and grabbed fistfuls of the comforter. How could she do this? She betrayed their trust so badly, how was she even capable? And then it dawned on her. Layla had her phone. She turned wild eyes up to Maddie, who had just entered the room, and yelled, "She has her phone!"

"What? Val, are you okay?"

Val shook her head and signaled for Maddie to wait. Her fingers shook as she opened the tracking app, and there, blinking on the screen like a beacon, was Layla's location.

In freaking Denver.

"You have to be kidding me!"

"What is going on?" Maddie asked.

"She's in Denver!" A billion questions flooded her mind. How did she get there? Who was she with? What the hell was she doing an hour away from home? In the city? She pulled up her contacts and dialed Layla's number. As expected, it went straight to voicemail. Val hung up and slammed the phone onto her bed.

Maddie reached out and settled her hands on Val's shoulders. "Breathe, Val."

A frustrated groan escaped her lips, but she complied. Val closed her eyes and took a deep breath, held it for a few counts, and finally let it all go. It would be okay. They knew where she was, and they would go down and get her.

"I have to call Peter."

Maddie stepped back. "I'm going to make us some tea."

"Have you reached any of her friends?" Peter said by way of a greeting.

"No. She took her phone out of my closet."

Peter didn't say anything. Val could almost hear him run his hand down his face, as stressed out as she was.

"I tracked it. She's in Denver." Val smoothed a finger over her eyebrow, doing her best to keep a tension headache from coming on. "She didn't answer when I called. Peter, what is she doing all the way down there?"

"I don't know." He heaved out a breath. "But at least we know where she is. Text her and tell her to stay put. I'm on my way to get her."

"If you pick me up, I could go with you."

"I just got out of the canyon, it'll be faster if I hop on Route 36 now. Just stay put. I've got her."

• • • •

MADDIE HAD FORCED VAL to sit down, covered her up with a blanket, and shoved a cup of tea into her hands. Rupa came barreling through the door moments later.

"I told you not to come," Val said.

Rupa wrapped an arm around Val. "I took a play from your book and decided not to listen."

"Thank you." Val leaned into her and closed her eyes.

"Peter's on his way. She'll be fine," Maddie said, taking a seat across from her.

Layla might be fine, but would Val ever be fine again? The anxiety of the last few hours shaved years off her life, she was sure of it.

"Did you ever run away?" Val asked, glancing between the two women, desperate for someone to tell her that this happens, it's just normal teenage stuff.

Maddie stared at the mug in her hands. "No. I was more of a good girl." Of course she was.

"I ran away once," Rupa said.

"Really?"

"Yeah. I was fifteen. My parents grounded me for something stupid that I can't even remember now. I was pissed, so I stuffed my backpack full of clothes and granola bars and snuck out while they were watching the nightly news."

Maddie's eyes went wide, and Val turned to her friend. "And?"

"My brother was driving home from a game and saw me sobbing along the side of the road. It was so dark, I had tripped on a rock and busted my ankle. He took me home, my parents grounded me for another week, and I never did it again. I mean, I couldn't, my leg was in a cast."

They all chuckled. If Val had run away, there wouldn't have been anyone around to notice. Her heart squeezed.

"When Layla comes back, she's going to feel stupid, I'm sure. I wouldn't be too hard on her," Rupa said. "Being a teenager sucks, and on top of that, a teenager with a uterus and all those swirling emotions."

Her phone buzzed. Peter.

"Did you find her?" Val could barely breathe.

"I'm fine, Mom." The sound of Layla's voice opened the floodgates, her heart exploding with relief. "I'm sorry." Layla's voice cracked, and they cried together.

• • • •

VAL'S FEET CRUNCHED against the gravel of Peter's driveway, her legs wobbly. Snow had begun to fall on their way up the canyon, a dusting already covering the sidewalk. When she reached the door, she turned and waved to Maddie and Rupa, who had insisted on driving her. And given the state she was in, Val was eternally grateful.

Peter answered the door, his face more haggard than usual. But goddamn it, no amount of stress could undo this man's supreme posture. Val stood there like a withered gremlin, shoulders hunched and her back full of knots. Peter raked a hand down his face and leaned on the doorframe.

"I told you not to come," he said.

"And I told you that I needed to see her." She pushed her way past him into the living room. Exposed wood and a vaulted ceiling gave the place a luxury cabin feel. Well, at least he could afford to give his next wife alimony since Val had never asked for it. Though it would have certainly come in handy, now that she thought about it.

Peter sighed and closed the door behind her. "Look, it's late. She needs to rest. You can stay in the guest room if you want, but we're not getting into it tonight."

Didn't he know that wouldn't cut it? Val had carried that little human inside her own body and thought tonight that she'd lost her. She couldn't stand to be even five miles away. "I just need to see her."

"She's probably asleep by now. Please don't interrogate her tonight. We can do that in the morning when we're all rested."

"What if she sneaks out again?" Val couldn't push her panic away. If she could, she would crawl into bed with Layla and hold her hand as she slept. Just to be sure she was there.

"She won't."

"Did she tell you what happened? Do you know why she did this?"

He sighed. "Yes, we talked in the car. Listen, I'm just as upset as you, but confronting her now isn't going to do anyone any good. She feels guilty enough as it is."

Peter was right, and if she had any amount of energy left in her, Val would have fought him on it, anyway, but all the worry and fear exhausted her to the bone.

She dropped her bag on the floor and slumped onto the sofa. "Fine. I just can't believe she would hop on a bus to Denver. Alone. What was she thinking?"

Peter sat next to her. "Can I say something?"

"God, I hate when people ask that. What am I going to say? No? Just say it." Val heaved a sigh and threw her head back against the sofa. Peter didn't say anything for a moment, and Val kicked herself for being such a dick. Of course this whole thing hadn't happened to just her. She wasn't the only one stressed out with worry. "I'm sorry."

"Maybe you push Layla too much," Peter said.

"What do you mean? Asking her to take care of her dishes or clear the fire hazards from her room qualify as pushy?"

"You showed up to her debate, even though you knew she didn't want that. You made a doctor's appointment for her against her wishes." He ticked these off on his fingers one by one, and it was certainly possible that he had enough grievances locked and loaded for all his digits, but Val couldn't deal with the accusations right now.

"You're right! I show up for her. I'm her mother. All I want is what's best for her."

He scratched the back of his neck, and his mouth did that twitchy thing that meant he had something to say but didn't know how she'd react.

"What?"

"What if what's best for her is a little space from you?"

The words slapped her in the face. Why would Layla need space from her? What did Peter know anyway?

"You've been trying so hard to not become your mother. You don't want Layla to feel neglected, but smothering her isn't the answer."

"What the hell? I'm just trying to give her something I didn't have. A mother who's there. That's not smothering!"

"All this anger you're holding, this resentment that you have. For me, your mom. It's affecting your relationship with your daughter. Can't you see?"

Val didn't want to. If she did, she would have to confront the feelings she had buried that were forcing their way up, burning the back of her eyes. She swallowed hard and blinked them away. It was easier to be angry.

"What does that have to do with this?" she asked.

"Layla doesn't trust you. You fly off the handle at the slightest provocation, and you're writing made-up bullshit." He picked up a copy of *Mile High Magazine* and smacked it on the table for emphasis.

Val closed her eyes and kicked herself. Of course Peter would read her work, he always had.

Dinner had been forgotten in the panic of the evening, and her head squeezed its announcement of an oncoming migraine. She needed to lie down.

"It's no wonder Layla doesn't trust you. You'd rather concoct a ridiculous story about a dying dog than confront your feelings about your dying mother." His voice held no accusation, just heaps of exhausted disappointment. And why shouldn't he be disappointed? Instead of taking an opportunity to grow up and learn something, she took the coward's way out. And what did that show Layla?

She was the asshole here, and everyone knew it.

Chapter 29

Val woke with a start, her heart racing. Sweaty sheets stuck to her back and legs. The night had been fitful, her brain full of worry and fear, but she must have slept, at least a little. As she pushed the duvet off her toasty body, the cool morning air rushed over her, instantly replacing beads of sweat with goose bumps.

Peter's guest room doubled as his yoga space, the day bed pushed up against the wall to allow enough room for a few people to fully stretch their bodies out across the floor. A large picture window took up an entire wall with sunlight streaming in and bouncing off the crisp eggshell paint, creating a sort of glow. Calming, refreshing. This would normally annoy Val to no end because, of course Peter's space looked like this. Stupidly perfect. But today, she was eternally grateful to have an uncluttered, tranquil place to rest after the stressful night they had.

Would she use the yoga mat rolled up in the corner? No, she most certainly would not. She wasn't feeling *that* Zen.

As she pulled on the clothes she had hastily shoved into her bag before leaving the house, she considered Peter's words from last night. She had every right to be upset at Layla for sneaking out and scaring them all half to death, but today was the day for listening. They would work out a plan together. But first, breakfast.

By the time Val made it into the kitchen, Peter had bacon sizzling and coffee perking. An old college sweatshirt hung over his lean frame, his long hair pulled into a ponytail, swinging just above his shoulders. He smiled at Val and gestured to a stool where a glass of water and a freshly peeled orange sat waiting for her. A warmth filled her chest. She had been nothing but a straight-up bitch to this man for years, and here he was, serving her breakfast like he did when they were first married.

A sense of longing pulled at her heart.

Not for Peter. Sure, she had loved him once, but she didn't want him back. What she missed was this casual familiarity with another person. To know what they liked to eat in the morning or how they took their coffee. Maybe she was ready to date, after all.

"How'd you sleep?" he asked as he flipped the pancake he had been watching over.

"Well, that's not an awful room you have back there." She popped a slice of orange into her mouth and savored the tangy juice, waking up her taste buds. "Listen, I thought more about what you said—"

"Mom? What are you doing here?" Layla trudged into the kitchen, her hair piled into a messy bun on top of her head. Puffy half moons sat below her bloodshot eyes. The sight of her yanked Val's heart out of her chest. She launched herself off the barstool and wrapped her in the tightest hug imaginable. Tears pricked at her eyes, and she didn't even bother blinking them back.

"You scared me half to death," Val cried into Layla's shoulder.

Layla squeezed her back, and time stood still. All the hugs they shared over their lifetime merged into this one embrace. Val clutched the toddler who had fallen after taking her first steps, held the small child who only wanted to spend all day sitting in Val's lap, and clung to the young girl who greeted her after school every day with a big smile and a giant squeeze.

Val didn't ever want to let go.

But Layla wasn't a little girl anymore. She was nearly a grown woman, and Val didn't need to hang on so tight. Shouldn't hang on so tight.

Val reluctantly pulled away and held Layla out at arm's length. She brushed a stray curl from Layla's eyes and resisted the urge to plant kisses all over her face.

"Why don't you both sit down?" Peter said, breaking them up. "Let's talk while we eat. And then we'll take you to school, okay?"

Peter dished up a plate of bacon, pancakes, and eggs for the two of them. It was not the diner fare Val was used to from The Greasy Spoon. Made from scratch from a hippie woo-woo man, there was certainly an inordinate amount of love and care that went into this meal, which made Val's heart melt a little.

What was happening to her?

"What is this, like, some last meal before you ground me for life?" Layla slumped in her seat, but the hard expression she usually wore was missing today. It had been replaced with what Val could only describe as remorse, guilt. Maybe even relief.

"No, honey," Peter said, patting Layla's leg. "We're just here to understand."

Val let Layla get a couple of bites in before speaking. She had to restrain herself from hitting Layla with a barrage of questions.

Listen.

"Layla, what happened last night?" She surprised herself with the lack of judgment that came with this question. Just a few days ago, Val would have exploded with accusations, which would have certainly ended in slammed doors and excessive grounding. Was it Peter's feng shui setup? Did she somehow achieve a calm yogi centering by osmosis?

"My friend was in trouble. I was just trying to help him," Layla said, her eyes focused on the plate in front of her.

"Yeah, I'm going to need more than that," Val said, unconvinced.

Layla poked at her pancakes with her fork, refusing to meet Val's gaze. "Dillon."

"Dillon?" She ran away with Dillon? Val had been worried about them spending time together, but she never thought Layla would attempt to run away with him. All this time they had been sneaking around. If only she had kept that Planned Parenthood appointment.

"It's not what you think." This time, Layla looked up, her eyes shiny and wet. "He's gay. And his dad is a real dick about it." A tear escaped, rolling down her cheek. "I didn't run away, Mom. He did. And he was scared. I just wanted to make sure he was okay. I was going to come back, I promise."

The words poured out of her like she couldn't hold them in any longer. Val's heart squeezed at the sight of Layla in pain. She had to swallow hard around the lump in her throat.

"Oh, honey, I had no idea," Val said, rubbing slow circles on Layla's back. "Why didn't you tell me?"

"What were you going to do, drive me down there to see him? You met him for a second and assumed he was trying to get in my pants."

The memory of that day at the mall came back to her. Hiding behind lacy lingerie to spy on her daughter. And the time in the bookstore, which looking back now, was just an innocent meeting of friends who cared deeply for each other. And Val had reacted as she always did. On impulse. No wonder Layla hadn't shared any of this with her until now.

"I don't know why you're so scared about me having sex. Because I'm not!"

"I just don't want you to do anything you might regret."

The scraping of Layla's fork against her plate cut through the silence.

Peter cleared his throat. "Maybe it's time to tell her."

Layla's head snapped up. "Tell me what?"

Val wiped her palms on her pants. It was time, and she knew that, but it didn't make it any easier. She turned to Layla and let out a breath. "Your dad and I were high school sweethearts, you knew that, right?"

"Yeah, so?"

"Well, we stopped being sweethearts when I got pregnant."

Layla's face scrunched up like it did whenever she had a complicated math problem to solve.

"Not with you, honey."

"You had another baby?"

Val shook her head. "No. I didn't have the baby. We were far too young and stupid to bring a baby into the world, we knew that at least."

"So you had an abortion?"

"Yeah. And I don't regret that at all, it was the right decision. I just don't want you to have to be in that situation, having to make that choice."

"Mom," Layla's voice was barely above a whisper. "You have to stop worrying about that. I'm not ready for sex, okay? And trust me, I know way more about birth control than you do."

Val met Peter's gaze from across the kitchen counter, and they shared a smile. She was right, of course. With information at her fingertips and a generation much more open to even talking about sex, she certainly had a leg up.

"Right. But sneaking out of the house when you were grounded? Stealing your phone out of my closet? Layla, you just can't do that."

"I know, but it was an emergency. I should have told you, I'm sorry." Layla hung her head, and Val thought she might cry again. She didn't think she could handle any more tears.

"Is Dillon okay?" Val asked.

Peter nodded. "His mom is in Denver, so we dropped him off before coming home."

"I wasn't running away from home," Layla said, looking straight at Val. "You can be so overbearing sometimes, but I wouldn't do that."

Val grabbed Layla's hand and squeezed. Her voice shook when she spoke again. "Let's make a pact. No more lies, no more skipping school, and I'll back off, okay?"

A single tear rolled down Layla's face, but she smiled. "Yeah, that's a great idea."

• • • •

THE DRIVE OUT OF THE canyon was silent with Peter at the wheel expertly guiding his Prius around the bends. Snow from last night covered the branches of the pines, the frost shimmery in the morning sunlight. It was like driving through a magical forest, which Val would appreciate more if she weren't so emotionally drained.

After dropping Layla off at school, Peter pulled up to Val's house. They sat for a moment, the car idling at the curb.

"Well, that was quite a night, wasn't it?" he said.

"Yeah, yeah, yeah, we both know you were the hero and saved the day." Val rolled her eyes, but the fight in her was gone.

"You don't have to do that, you know," he said softly.

Val turned to him. His attention stayed on the steering wheel. "Do what?"

He finally met her gaze, his eyes shiny and red-rimmed. "Verbally attack. We're divorced, and co-parenting is hard, but that doesn't mean we have to fight every time we talk. It's exhausting, and I'd rather not do it."

It was at this moment that Val realized that she never actually had a sparring partner. All her verbal spats with Peter had been one-sided. He hadn't done anything to egg her on, didn't pull out any swords or guns. She was the only one who had been armed. That fact squeezed her heart and simultaneously flooded her with relief. Being defensive all the time wasn't a way to live. And she was tired of doing it.

Val nodded slowly. "You're right." She turned to him, the heaviness of the last fourteen hours etched all over his stubbly face. "Can I still make fun of you?"

This won her a smile. "Wait, you make fun of me?" His tone was serious, but mischief danced in his eyes.

She chucked him lightly on the arm before opening the door. Halfway out of the car, Val paused, turning back to Peter.

"Thank you," she said, genuinely meaning it this time.

An understanding passed between them. They had reached new territory. After a year of wading through a swamp together, they were finally on dry land. A fresh start.

Chapter 30

"Where's Valerie?" her mother asked, shuffling over to the window. "I have something for her."

Val was about to correct her but then thought better of it. No need to create a scene, she'd just gotten here, after all. It had been weeks since Val had come for a visit, but something pulled her here today. All the emotions that had been stirred up when Layla ran away had her just wanting to see her mom.

"Valerie couldn't come today." Her mother's face fell, and her shoulders slumped. So Val quickly added, "But I can give it to her. Whatever it is that you have."

Her mom pondered this for a moment before nodding. "Yes, will you?"

Val studied her, shoulder bones protruding through her sweater, her spine curled in on itself. She had been so much more, once upon a time. Val recalled a framed photo of her mother in her twenties and how she used to sneak into her mother's room to study that photograph.

Her mother had been young and happy, arms spread wide on top of a mountain she had just spent hours trekking up. Snowcaps on all sides proved how high she climbed, and her face oozed with pride at her accomplishment. Val had loved this glossy version of her mother. When had she become this shriveled up shadow of herself?

Her mother turned back to Val with a notebook in her hands. And it took a minute for Val to understand that it was *that* notebook. The gold notebook she used to write in when she was young. The one she hadn't seen in decades.

"I wanted to give this back to her," she said, handing it to Val.

Val took it in her hands, caressing the raised hearts that sprung from the binding. "Where did you get this, Mom?" Val whispered, her voice full of awe.

Her mother hooked Val's elbow with one arm and steadied herself on her cane. Val led her back to her chair.

"I've been hanging on to it for her."

"Why?"

"Valerie is so smart and talented. She's going to be a brilliant writer someday, I just know it."

Val's chest expanded until she thought it might burst. "Really?"

Her mom patted her arm and nodded. "This is the first story she wrote." She looked up at Val, her eyes shiny with tears. "It's about us."

The vise around Val's chest tightened ever so slightly. She could remember writing in it and loving every minute of it, but had she written about her mother?

How did her mom even have this? Val was certain she went through all her mom's stuff before moving her into the facility. With Peter's help, they had gotten rid of almost everything, setting aside a few boxes of keepsakes. How did this slip through?

"Will you have her finish it? For me? I always wanted to know how it was going to end."

Val swallowed hard around the lump in her throat and could do nothing but nod.

Chapter 31

"Okay, you win!" Val said, barging into Evelyn's office with a huff. She had spent all night reading the notebook her mother gave her, and she finally had some stuff to talk about.

"Excuse me?"

Val slapped the notebook down on the coffee table and dropped into the chair opposite Evelyn. "Let's talk about her."

Evelyn raised her eyebrows a fraction of an inch and said nothing. The woman was a goddamn mannequin.

"My mother. You've been dying to hear about her, so let's get into it."

And so Val did. She recounted all the times her mother had chosen a mani/pedi or cocktails with friends over being with her. Of the times her mother had forgotten her birthday or made her feel like an afterthought. And then Val told Evelyn, in detail, of the day she had an abortion. Alone.

"Had you told your mother that you were pregnant?" Evelyn asked after listening to Val spill her guts for twenty minutes straight.

"No." Val picked at a hole in her jeans. "I wanted to tell her. I tried to. But she was always coming home late or brushing me off." Making herself remember this tugged at her heart, and she felt sorry for the sad teenager who hadn't known how to handle such a grown-up situation.

"I made the appointment myself, but they wanted someone to be there with me. You know, to drive me home. I told them that she was coming to pick me up, thinking that she would if I just called her. But when I did call, she couldn't be bothered. Said she was busy and to take the bus. So I rode the bus. Bleeding, nauseous, and in need of...well, my mom."

After a long pause, Evelyn leaned forward in her chair, her penetrating gaze so full of empathy and compassion that tears sprang to

Val's eyes instantly. She wasn't used to this level of understanding from Evelyn. Or anyone, really.

"That must have been scary," Evelyn said softly.

"She didn't even stay on the phone long enough for me to tell her what had happened. She didn't care." Truth was, she probably had a martini in front of her that was more important.

"I'm so sorry that happened to you," Evelyn said. "And now you're caring for your mother when she wasn't there to care for you."

"Yeah."

"That must be hard."

"A kick in the crotch, actually." Val sighed, a weight freeing from her chest. Why had this been so hard to talk about?

Evelyn sat back in her chair and eyed the notebook on the table. "Want to talk about that?"

Did she? It almost seemed silly now, after unloading years of teenage grievances, to discuss the strange love story she had started writing so many years ago. A story filled with little anecdotes about growing up with her mom. Cooking together in the kitchen, playing games, telling jokes, and watching movies together. How they had laughed and shared secrets like they had been best friends. The movies, she remembered, but everything else? Had she written a fictional story about them? About the world she wished she lived in? Or had Val remembered it all differently?

It didn't even matter anymore. Her mother didn't remember any of this anyway. What good would it do to keep hanging on to the past?

Shaking her head, Val picked up the notebook and tucked it into her bag.

Evelyn looked at her thoughtfully. "I think, for your last assignment, I'd like for you to consider offering forgiveness."

And just as Val had feared, this assignment turned out to be the hardest one yet.

Chapter 32

The house was quiet with Layla at Peter's place. They all agreed it would be better for her to be sequestered there for a while. Quiet, peaceful, no easy access to her friends or bus routes and, most importantly, a break from her mother.

It had hurt knowing that Layla needed to get out from under her nose. But now that they figured out the problem, they could work on repairing their relationship. Val just needed to learn how to back off and give her some space. She could do that, right?

With an approaching deadline, Val opened her laptop, ready to hammer out her next article for the magazine. But things had changed. She no longer wanted to write something fake for show. While misleading her readers, Sonia, and everyone else at the office had felt like the only way to go to keep her job at the time, it now seemed trivial and pointless. And exhausting. She couldn't possibly conjure up another fake story if she tried. She just didn't have the energy.

But she'd have to find something quick because there was something she needed to do.

• • • •

"HEY," VAL CROUCHED down next to Maddie's desk the next morning. "I need you to be my emotional support person for a minute."

Maddie turned to her. "Anything! What do you need?"

Of course Maddie would so valiantly offer herself up and help Val out, which strengthened her resolve. She needed to do this. It had only been one day since spilling her guts to Evelyn, but that meeting had changed everything.

"Come with me, please." Val stood and motioned for Maddie to follow.

"Where are we going?"

Val gave a small smile and knocked on Sonia's office door. She could feel Maddie stiffen next to her, so she gave her arm a little pat. "Don't worry, it's fine."

"Come in," Sonia called.

Val wiped her sweaty palms on her jeans and pushed the door open. She could do this. She had to do this.

Sonia looked up from her laptop and smiled at the two of them. "Maddie. Val. What can I do for you?"

Taking one of the chairs on the other side of Sonia's desk, Val motioned for Maddie to sit down. Maddie glanced between the two of them, her eyes full of suspicion. Fair. Val deserved all the suspicion and doubt Maddie threw her way. She would never trust Val again after this.

Sonia leaned on her desk and steepled her fingers, her eyebrows suggesting Val get a move on and say something.

"Well," Val said, fiddling her thumbs. Nice one. Great start. "I want to say thank you, Sonia. For giving me a second chance and offering me the features column. I really appreciate that."

Val shifted in her seat. Why was this so hard?

Sonia smiled. "And?"

"And I truly don't deserve it. Maddie is the one who deserves that column."

"Val," Maddie whispered, "what are you doing?"

Ever the professional, Sonia said nothing. Goddamn her and her silences. She would have made a great therapist.

"It's just that, when you fired me," Val continued, "I deserved that. I had been doing a terrible job, I know."

"Val, we have a major deadline to meet today, so get to your point."

"Right." Val cleared her throat. "The idea that I pitched about self-improvement? It wasn't mine. It was all Maddie. Hell, she even wrote it up and sent it to you."

Maddie leaned forward in her seat, her gaze cast to the floor, worrying at the hem of her shirt. Val hadn't considered that this confession would get Maddie in trouble, but now she was concerned she had overstepped and should have just left Maddie out of this. She rushed to repair the damage.

"She was looking out for me, just being a good friend. I'm sorry I took the idea as my own. I should have told you from the beginning."

Sonia leaned back in her chair. "I don't know what to say."

"Well, before you say anything, just know that I'm stepping down. I wanted to thank you again for the opportunity, and I really think Maddie should have the spot. She's got great ideas, this being one of them."

"But, Val, this is all you," Maddie said. "I may have suggested it, but it's the work you're currently doing. It's your story."

Val hung her head, ashamed. "It's not. I've been making it all up."

"What?" Sonia and Maddie said in unison.

"I was just writing letters I thought our readers could connect with. I was pretending to be vulnerable." She wanted the ground to swallow her whole so she could stop broadcasting what an idiot she was.

"What about Gladys?" Sonia's voice held a hopeful note, as if maybe, just maybe, Val wasn't a horrible monster and the dog had been real.

Val didn't look up. She pinched her lips together and shook her head.

Maddie gasped, her hand reaching her throat. "You made up Gladys?" Of all the things Val had pulled out of thin air, of course Maddie would be most upset about an imaginary dog.

"You told me to change some things—"

"I said to change the names, not create a work of fiction!" Maddie crossed her arms and stared out the window. "I can't believe you."

It shouldn't be possible to feel like a bigger piece of shit than she already did, but hearing Maddie's tone of voice, shame coursed through her. She was in the principal's office being scolded for making poor choices. But at least she could own up to them now.

"Let me get this straight." This time, Sonia's voice was hard as stone. "You lied to me. And you lied to our readers?"

"I lied to everyone. To myself." Val hung her head. This couldn't get any more humiliating. "I'm sorry. You don't have to fire me, I quit. I just have a favor to ask."

It all seemed like a good idea in her head, this one last request. But Sonia glared in her direction, and Maddie's eyes filled with such horror, as if Val had killed a puppy instead of made one up, that Val could no longer be sure. Maybe Sonia would kick her out of the office, and honestly, it was what she deserved. But she got up the courage to ask anyway.

This needed to be done.

Chapter 33

Val hit send on her latest and final submission for the magazine. How Sonia had the capacity for enough forgiveness to allow her to write one more article, she'd never know. But it was done and would be published for the world to see in exactly one week. How people would take it, she wasn't sure. Maybe she'd be ostracized, the dog lovers of the community could picket outside her house. Or maybe no one would read it or actually care. Only time would tell.

Maddie hadn't responded to any of her text messages, but that was no surprise. Lying to help a friend and lying for some self-preservation were two different things, apparently.

But now that was done, it was time to move on to Evelyn's assignment. Making amends. Which she technically just did for her readers, but it wasn't enough.

She knew exactly who to make amends with, but how can you do that with a person who doesn't remember you? Not really, anyway. To her mother, Val was still a teenager, having given up on getting her attention altogether.

But she had to try.

Val flipped the notebook to a fresh page, grabbed a pen, and did her best to steady her hand. She took a deep breath and poured her heart out onto the page.

A half hour and many tissues later, it was down on paper. Val carefully tore the pages out of her notebook, folded them, and tucked them into an envelope. She had written so many letters that no one else would ever read, but this one was priority mail to be hand delivered. And now that it was all on paper and out of her heart, she felt a pull to deliver it as soon as possible.

Before it was too late.

She stole a glance at her watch. If she hurried, she could make it before visiting hours were over. They had waited long enough as it was, this had to be done now. Man, she would have been roasted on a #AITA Reddit thread. Of course she was the asshole. In her mind, her mother abandoned her long ago to find herself. But really, as a single mom without any support system, her mom had just been doing her best. And it wasn't fair for Val to hold something over her head that wasn't even her fault. Her mom had no idea any of that had happened.

Evening traffic inched along, making her miss every single green light, and Val thought she might burst right out of her skin. Why this had suddenly become an emergency wasn't clear, but if Val didn't get there soon, she feared her blood pressure would rise high enough to pop the vessels in her eyes.

She was shaking with adrenaline by the time she pulled into the nursing home's parking lot, her head bursting with memories of her mother. Not ones of her getting ignored or being pushed away, but of ones where her mother was doing the best with what she had. Where she loved Val enough to work so hard to provide a good life for them both. Where she took the time to care for herself so that she could be a better parent.

And all the times she was just human.

A mother who made mistakes, no different from Val. And that thought hit her like a brick. *Layla*. She didn't deserve to carry Val's childhood baggage; they weren't the same.

Val sprang out of the car and checked the time just to be sure. Visiting hours would be over in ten minutes, but that was long enough for her to get this off her chest.

Her feet pounded the tile floor, echoing off the wall, in rhythm with her hurried heartbeat. She turned down the hall to the memory care unit, and the sight of Peter sitting on a chair outside her mother's room caused her to falter. He was leaning forward with his elbows on his knees, his fingers tapping together impatiently. What was he doing here?

"Peter?"

Peter turned to her and then leaped from the chair. He ran a hand down his face. "God, Val, where have you been?" He was agitated, that much was clear. But why?

"What do you mean? I've been at home, I—"

"Don't you ever answer your phone? I've been trying to reach you. The nurse has been trying to reach you."

Val's heart nosedived into the depths of her stomach. She had turned her phone on silent so she could work, and she must not have switched it back.

"What's going on? Is she okay?" Val pushed past Peter and stepped into the room.

Her mother's small body lay on the bed, motionless but for the occasional shallow breath. Wisps of hair barely covered her scalp, her cheeks hollowed to the point where she could be confused for Halloween décor.

She looked so much older than her seventy years. Val saw her just the other day, and she had been doing well. As well as she could have, anyway.

A nurse checked the drip that was attached to her mother's arm and looked up at Val with compassion. "We're just keeping her as comfortable as possible."

Val's legs were rooted to the spot, as if her feet had melted into the tile. This was it. She had finally come to say all the things her mother needed to hear, but it was too late?

"What...what happened?"

The nurse touched Val's arm and smiled sympathetically. "Just normal progression of the disease, I'm afraid."

Sensing Val's immobility, she cupped her elbow and led Val to the chair next to the bed.

"While we're not sure if she can hear you at this point, I like to believe she can. Talk to her, I'll give you some space." She patted Val's shoulder and left the room.

Val took in the sight of her mother and could barely catch her breath. Her mom was dying. She had been aware of this since the diagnosis came, but to see it happen with her own two eyes wasn't something she had expected. She wasn't sure she could handle it.

Peter walked over and placed a hand on her shoulder. "I'm so sorry, Val."

"I wrote her a letter." The words just fell out of her mouth. She held up the letter as if she had to prove to him that it was true. Peter gave her shoulder a squeeze but said nothing. "I just finally had stuff I wanted to say." She blinked fast, but it was no use, hot tears cascaded down her cheeks.

"Read it to her. I'll be in the hall if you need me." Another shoulder squeeze, and he was gone.

Val sat for a moment, unable to move. Her mother's body had shriveled to nothingness, nearly swallowed up by blankets. Val wouldn't have been surprised if she turned to dust right before her eyes.

And then her focus came back to the envelope in her hand, the very reason she was here right now. She unfolded the letter, her hands trembling.

"Hi, Mom," she whispered. It felt weird, speaking to this shell of a human. Most of her mind had left her years ago, who knew what was left. And what did this matter, anyway?

But it did matter. Val had clung to a resentment for so long that only proved to wreak havoc on the rest of her life. She needed to let it go.

She stared at the letter. The words on the page were written from a younger version of Val. Of a teenage Valerie, the person her mother remembered. Airing her grievances, apologizing for not demanding her attention and standing up for herself. But Val couldn't read those words. She wasn't that kid any longer.

Val dropped the letter in her lap and took her mom's delicate hand in hers, the paper-thin skin cold to the touch.

"Mom, I..." Why was this so hard? She was barely here, Val could say anything she wanted to, and no one would know. Not even her mother. So why couldn't she just say it?

"You weren't there for me. I can list all the times that I needed you and you weren't there. I felt unloved." Only now that she said the word out loud did it ring true. She wiped her cheeks.

"But if you had a chance to do it over again, I believe you'd make different choices because I know I would." So many things she'd redo if she could. From decisions she made being young and reckless to everything after that.

One would think that turning older guaranteed a bit more wisdom, but Val had been screwing up left and right as time went on.

"I forgive you." And this, Val knew wasn't something her mother needed. Val never had to forgive her if she didn't want to. But to heal and move forward, this was something she needed to do. For herself.

And with those words, Val let go of her mother. Of the one who hadn't been around growing up and the glossy version, all smiles and joy on top of that mountain. The mother Val wished she had been and this shell of a person, who hadn't really been her mother at all.

It was at that moment that her mother must have had the same idea, to let it all go. As Val sat there, clutching her hand, her mother let out her last breath.

Chapter 34

The week following her mother's passing had been filled with phone calls, paperwork, and cleaning out her room at the nursing home. Val had been grateful to have an empty house in which to crash at the end of the day, physically and emotionally exhausted from it all. She didn't have to keep it together for Layla or anyone else.

Val reached The Greasy Spoon for their weekly breakfast date, fully prepared for Maddie to ghost her, but clinging to some hope that she would be there, and they could talk this out. As she peered in the window, her gaze caught on Maddie, perched on a barstool, with Barb as her captivated audience.

A couple left the building, and Val snagged the door before it could hit the chimes again. She wanted the element of surprise, but before she made it to the counter, Maddie's excited voice caught her attention.

"'These articles were supposed to be a way to show you how I can be vulnerable and take my life and my healing into my own hands. Instead, I used this as a joke.'"

Holy shit, she was reading Val's article. Out loud!

"'I deliberately deceived you and tricked you all into believing that I was working on my anger, my past trauma, my grief. When in reality, I was just using it as an excuse to have this job. I wanted to write this column so bad that I was willing to tell you lies about myself.'"

Heat crept up Val's neck. She couldn't stand it any longer, she didn't need to hear the drawn-out apology spoken aloud.

"Hey," she said, grabbing a seat next to Maddie.

Maddie spun around with a surprised "Eep!" before she sprung off the stool and wrapped her noodly arms around Val, bouncing her back and forth. "Valerie I-don't-know-your-middle-name Knight! I loved it! It was so perfect!"

Val grabbed Maddie's wrist and tried to wrench herself free. "I'm going to bounce right off this stool if you don't let go."

Maddie gave one more squeeze before landing back on her seat.

"You're not mad anymore?" Val couldn't help but ask. Just a few months ago and she wouldn't have cared, but now? She cared a whole helluva lot.

"You made a mistake, and you owned up to it." Maddie's eyes filled with tears. "I'm just so proud of you."

Maddie threw her arms around Val, and the weight she had walked in with alleviated.

"At first, I thought you were bonkers. Like you had lost your ever-loving mind, for real this time. I couldn't believe you would give up your column after you fought so hard to get it back. And your article!" Maddie made the universal sign for a brain explosion, her smile growing even wider. "You were so open and honest." Maddie held her phone to her chest and beamed.

Val cleared her throat. "Well, yes, I was more honest. But there are some things I didn't want to air publicly. But given that you are my friend, you are deserving of the truth."

Maddie listened while Val spent the next ten minutes filling her in on her mother. Val had kept her out of the article because the public didn't need to know everything.

"Oh my gosh, Val, I'm so sorry." Maddie swiped at her face. "Why didn't you ever say anything? I would have been there for you, I hope you know that."

"I know that now." Val squeezed Maddie's hand. "What can I say, I'm still a work in progress."

"Well, I'm bringing you and Layla dinner tomorrow, and I won't take no for an answer."

Val just smiled.

"Oh, I need to thank you," Maddie said, squeezing Val's hand right back. "Sonia turned the column over to me."

The old Val might feel jealous, or maybe a bit angry at this. But the new and improved Val felt nothing but love and joy for this incredible woman.

"And you'll do amazing," Val said, truly meaning it.

Without being asked, Barb placed a coffee mug in front of Val and poured the diner's infamous brew. She winked at Val before heading into the dining area. Huh. Miracles never cease.

"So," Maddie said, bringing Val's attention back to her. "What are you going to do now?"

The million-dollar question. She had been toying with the idea of finally finishing that story, the one she started so long ago. The one her mother requested she finish. It felt like the right time to work on a love story between a mother and daughter, but how she was going to make it happen was a bit unclear.

For Maddie, she just shrugged and said, "I'll think of something."

"Freelance?"

Val grimaced. "Never again."

Maddie hooked an arm around her shoulder and squeezed. "Well, whatever it is you decide to do, I fully support you."

When they had finished their coffee, Val grabbed the check from Maddie. "My treat." She didn't have much of her last paycheck left, but what she did have was going to be spent wisely.

She pulled some bills from her wallet and handed them to Barb, along with the check.

"Keep the change."

She smiled, a true, genuine smile. Not a snarky, sarcastic one. Flinging her purse strap over her head, she skirted to the door before Barb could find the hundred-dollar bill. The woman might be a constipated ass sometimes, but who wasn't?

• • • •

A FEW WEEKS LATER, Val found herself sitting across from Evelyn once more, but this time, she actually wanted to be there.

"Well," Evelyn said, her face ever the same: a small smile and friendly eyes that gave away absolutely nothing. "This is our last court-ordered visit. Congratulations."

"It is?" Val said, her voice full of wonder, although she had been counting down these sessions since they began. She might even have placed a gigantic red star next to this appointment on her calendar. Party balloons, champagne toasts, all the celebratory emojis. And it was a celebration of sorts. Val had her breakthrough, but she didn't need Evelyn to tell her that.

"Here's the thing," Val said, leaning her elbows on her knees and tapping her fingers together. "I don't want this to be my last session. For the courts, yes, god, yes! But I would like to still come and see you. If that's okay."

There wasn't a lot that gave Val apprehension, but waiting for Evelyn to respond to her request absolutely did. She hadn't realized how much she needed Evelyn until now. And now that she could tell she was on an upswing, she didn't want to let her go.

A small smile spread on Evelyn's face, but the look in her eyes could have meant anything. Joy that she finally got through to someone so exhausting? Dread that she had to keep listening to her? Who's to say?

"It's perfectly okay. I'm glad to see that taking care of your mental health is a priority for you. Should we pick up where we left off last time?"

• • • •

VAL LEFT EVELYN'S OFFICE with an all-clear for the courts, a recurring appointment for herself, and a lightness in her chest.

She turned on the car, cranked the heat, and hammered out a quick text to Layla. They had agreed to no phone calls, but texting was fine, within limits. Val was trying to give Layla the space, even though it pained her to do so. But this, she also knew, was for the best.

Val: *I can't wait to have you back home this weekend. Want anything special for dinner?*

Two weeks at Peter's was too long for Val. She missed this awkward teenage daughter of hers. The attitude, the mess, and door slamming included. The house was too quiet without her.

Layla: *pizza?*

Val: *Hawaiian?*

Layla: *of course.*

Thank god none of Layla's pretentious friends had gotten to her yet about how gross everyone believed Hawaiian pizza to be. It was delicious.

Layla: *and a rom-com for family movie night?*

Val's heart leaped right out of her chest. And if it could have, it would have done some kick-ass celebratory street dancing. She clutched her phone to her chest, an overwhelming wave of emotion hitting her. God, she loved that kid.

Val: *Any movie you want.* ☺

• • • •

Chapter 35

I t was Friday, the day that Layla was due to be home. Val was swimming in emotions but tried her best to keep them in check. The last thing Layla needed was to come home to a weepy mess of a mom.

When Layla arrived home after school, Val was in the kitchen, baking up a batch of snickerdoodles. She had promised herself that she wouldn't be too clingy, that she would give Layla all the space she needed—within reason. But she had to make her favorite cookies.

She resisted the urge to lunge at Layla when she opened the front door. Her girl had grown in the two weeks she was gone. Every day, she was more and more a young woman, the little girl she once was a mere ghost.

"Hey, honey," Val said, rooted to her spot in the kitchen. If Layla wanted a hug, she would come get one, Val was not going to push. "It's good to see you."

Layla kicked off her shoes and dropped her backpack and coat onto the floor because, teenagers. "Smells good." She sauntered into the kitchen, and Val could no longer resist. She pulled Layla into a quick, side hug, hoping that would be okay.

Thankfully, Layla smiled and leaned into her. "I missed you, sweetie," Val whispered into her hair.

"Are you making snickerdoodles?" Layla stuck a finger into the bowl of batter and took a taste. Her eyes widened knowingly, and she leaned into Val again. "Thanks, Mom. I missed you, too." Val's chest squeezed.

Layla pulled a spoon out of the silverware drawer and dug into the batter. Val could hardly argue, it was the best way to enjoy a cookie. Smooth, raw, the danger of salmonella part of the thrill. They shared spoonfuls until their tummies ached.

"How's Dillon?" Val said.

Layla shrugged. "He's not going to live with his dad anymore, so that's good. His mom's great, but he misses it up here."

"What if he stayed with us next weekend?"

Layla's spoon clattered against the glass bowl. She turned to Val with wide eyes. "Are you serious?"

Val shrugged. "As long as this week goes well and you get your homework done, I don't see why not."

Layla threw her arms around Val. "Oh, Mom, thank you!"

Val squeezed her right back. "Speaking of homework, do you have any to do this weekend?"

Layla groaned. "Yeah, but I really don't want to do it."

"I know, but why don't you take some time now just to get it out of the way and then we can watch a movie and you can enjoy the rest of the weekend, you know?"

"Yeah, enjoy it grounded in my room?" There was the Layla that Val knew.

Val bobbed her head back and forth noncommittally and said, "I might have something planned."

. . . .

"MY FAVORITE PEOPLE!" Rupa sing-songed the next morning as she hugged Val around the middle. "I'm so glad we're doing this!"

"I'm not," Layla grumbled behind them, crunching through the darkened parking lot. It was far too early for any human to be up and walking around, but here they were.

Rupa turned and slung an arm over her shoulder. "Oh, kiddo, I'm so sorry to hear about Lulu."

Layla kicked at the dirt. "It's okay, she didn't really know me."

"Yeah, but it still sucks." Rupa wrapped Layla in a hug, resting her chin in Layla's curls. "Well, I'm so glad you're here." She kissed the top of her head. "You'd do anything for your mom, right?"

Val yawned, her brain still powered down for the night. "You make it sound like this was my idea."

Waking up at five a.m. in the middle of November to hike a mountain would never be her idea. Not in a million years. But Rupa had used all her annoying charm and convinced her it would be worth it. And even though Layla had complained about how she could see her breath, she ultimately couldn't refuse a chance to hang out with Rupa.

"I think you guys need some coffee, and then you'll be fine," Rupa said, handing them each a travel mug.

"I think you need some sleep," Val said, eyeing her friend in the light of the streetlamp. Her full face of makeup and long flowy dress peeking out of her jacket were certainly left over from last night's gig, but the hiking boots and cozy outerwear were donned specifically for this occasion.

Val sipped her coffee, desperate for a warmup, her stretchy gloves doing nothing to keep her fingers from turning to icicles.

Rupa had assured her that getting to the top in time for sunrise would be enough to energize her for the entire week. She'd see about that.

"How are we even going to see where we're going?" Layla asked, wiping the sleep out of her eyes. She had a point. The sky still clung to the darkness, the foothills in front of them giant, sleeping shadows.

"With these." Rupa handed out headlamps, and they all strapped them on.

"Ugh, I feel like a dork," Layla said, her beam of light aimed directly in Val's face. "Do I have to wear this?"

"Only if you want to see where you're going. The sun's not coming up for another..." Rupa checked her watch. "Oh! We have a little over an hour, so let's go!"

Rupa led them down the path past her apartment complex, through the neighborhood park, until they hit the trailhead. The air was still and quiet but for Rupa's humming and the sound of their feet crunching on the trail. Val adjusted the pack on her back, heavy with the pastries and fruit she promised Layla at the top.

"Mom said that hiking every day was *your* self-improvement challenge, why did you have to rope us into it?" Layla asked, still dragging her feet behind them.

Rupa laughed, the sound echoing in the quiet of the woods. "Because it's good for you! Besides, you'll thank me when you get to the top, I promise."

"Doubtful," Layla muttered.

Val hooked her arm in Layla's for a brief moment and whispered, "I needed you here to keep me company. I couldn't be left alone with this exercise freak."

"Do you think she's high?" Layla snickered.

"Wouldn't doubt it."

"I can hear you two!" Rupa swung around, her arms spread wide and her headlamp beaming up to the sky. "I'm just high on life, thank you very much. And I thought I could convince your mother to take on some outdoor activity for her next challenge."

Val scoffed. "One challenge is enough for me."

"And how's that one going?" Rupa asked.

Val hadn't written any letters since quitting the magazine, but she had a feeling anything she did write would finally make a difference. She might be taking baby steps to self-improvement, but that was all she needed.

"I'm getting there," she said.

They crunched along, their bodies warming up enough to take off the chill. After a while, the early morning light crept up from the ground, as if the sun was set with a dimmer switch, and they took off their headlamps.

By the time they reached the top, an orange glow had settled over the city below, lighting it on fire. The three of them stood in awe, Rupa with her arms spread wide and Val with her hand on her side, breathing away a cramp. When they finally caught their breath, Val pulled out their picnic breakfast, and they sat, watching the sunrise.

"Lulu would have loved this," Val said softly, picturing her mother on top of that mountain, her face full of joy.

"Really?" Layla said around a mouthful of bear claw.

"She was an outdoor enthusiast, once upon a time, anyway." Val pulled her phone out of her pocket and handed it to Rupa. "Take a picture of us?"

Layla swiped crumbs from her mouth and let Val pull her in close. They smiled for the camera, and Val couldn't resist bringing Layla in for a tight squeeze, kissing the top of her hat.

"I'm just so happy to have you home, honey."

Chapter 36

"So that's it?" Layla asked from the doorway, eyeing Val with suspicion. Coat zipped and boots on, she was clearly ready to brave the early round of snow they'd just received.

Val brought her cup of tea to her lips with a nonchalant shrug. "What do you mean?"

"You're not going to grill me? No twenty questions?" If Val didn't know any better, the look on Layla's face could have been confused with disappointment. But Val knew she was jumping with joy on the inside.

Val put her teacup on the side table and snuggled in deeper under the fleece blanket. "You're going out with friends, and why shouldn't you, you're on Thanksgiving break. That's fine." Val offered Layla a reassuring smile. "But it is my motherly duty to ask you to wear a hat. It's cold outside."

Layla rolled her eyes but didn't hesitate. She grabbed her hat and shoved it on her head.

"Happy?"

"Thrilled. Be home by ten."

It hadn't been easy getting here. To the place where Val could trust Layla (at least a little) and trust herself not to worry about her (at least not too much). But the small steps she'd taken over the last few weeks had done them both a world of good. And it would only get better from here, she could feel it.

Val contemplated how far she'd come over the last month. A new job, a new goal, and no massive screwups. Not anymore. With Evelyn's support and encouragement, she felt like a new person altogether. And her journey of self-improvement had never been about writing all those letters. Although she was still determined to finish, it had been about carving out some space to dig into herself.

And what had she learned in the process? More than she would have imagined. If only she would have realized it all when she was younger, life wouldn't have been so complicated.

Val opened her laptop and pulled up a new document. She had one more letter she needed to get off her chest before doing anything else.

It had been hard to forgive her mother and to let go of the resentment she had carried around for years, but doing so had been freeing in ways Val had never imagined. And there was one more person she wanted to extend that forgiveness to: herself.

Chapter 37

Six Months Later

Val loaded the conveyor belt with all the picnic goodies she could afford and tugged off her green apron. Her feet ached from being on them for the last six hours. It had been years since Val had worked retail, and she had forgotten how exhausting it could be. But taking the job at Whole Foods meant flexible hours, time to devote to her writing, and discounts on the best cheeses around. Besides, she said she would only stay until her book was finished, and Val had a feeling that was right around the corner.

"I didn't see you on the schedule for tomorrow," Ava complained as she scanned Val's purchases. Little heart stickers littered the name tag that sat askew on her shirt, reminding Val a bit of Layla. This must be why she liked her.

"I'm off the entire weekend. Tomorrow's my birthday," Val said. And this time around, Val didn't hate saying that. So she was closer to death, so what?

"Oh, Val, happy birthday!" Ava blew a bubble with her chewing gum and snapped it with her teeth. "Damn. Who's going to make fun of Brad with me tomorrow?"

Val touched her arm. "I believe in you. We close together on Monday, we can gang up on him then. Oh, I marked down your favorite brie and stuffed it under the clearance basket for you." She winked.

Ava sighed dramatically as only one in their early twenties could do. "How did you get to work with all the cheese?" She practically drooled over the smoked bacon gouda in her hands.

"I told them I grew up on a dairy farm in the Midwest."

Ava stopped scanning and cocked her head. "You grew up on a farm?"

Val just smiled. "Nope."

A fluorescent light overhead flickered, and the credit card machine beeped. Val stuffed her card back into her wallet and looped her reusable bag over her shoulder, giving Ava a little salute.

• • • •

ONCE HOME, VAL LOADED up the picnic basket. "Layla, grab your stuff, we've gotta get going." Rupa would be on stage for Music in the Park in less than an hour, but they needed to meet up with Peter first.

Layla skulked out of her room, a backpack resting on her shoulder and a hoodie covering half her face.

"Rough day?" Val asked.

Her question was met with an inarticulate grumble. Val passed her the picnic blanket, scooped up the rest of their stuff, and followed Layla outside.

"Any big plans this weekend? And don't say orgy, I can't handle it."

Layla shoved the blanket into the back of the car and climbed into the front seat. "Dillon's coming over."

"Oh, yeah?"

"Yeah. We're gonna get high and ponder the meaning of life."

"Oh, stop it!" Val lightly socked Layla in the arm. "You're the worst."

"I learn from the best," Layla said, finally tossing a smile her way.

• • • •

BY THE TIME THEY MADE it to the festival, the park teemed with couples and families, blankets and camping chairs dotting the grass. A warm breeze blew through, whipping her ponytail into her face.

"I see Dad," Layla said, waving to someone by the food trucks. "Ready for your hot date?"

Val turned to her. "I think so. How do I look?"

Layla scanned her classic INXS T-shirt and faded jeans, cuffed around the ankles. Her eyebrows rose, and she made that face that said maybe Val didn't want to know.

"Well?"

"You look...low-maintenance."

Val shrugged. "Eh. You're not wrong."

Layla's eyes softened. "This is the first one since Dad, right?"

"Yeah. So we'll see."

"Good for you. You'll do great."

Her chest filled with a bucket full of warm fuzzies. Val might not be even close to a good person, but she was raising a great one.

"Thanks, honey. I love you." Val opened her arms and took a step toward her, but Layla took a step back before her hug could land.

"Ugh, Mom, we're in public." Layla turned and walked in the direction of the food trucks, waving her goodbye.

Overwhelming pride washed through Val as she watched Layla walk away. She spied Peter in the distance and waved. He gave her a smile and waved back before attempting the same hug move on Layla, which she also rejected. Nice.

"They grow up so fast, don't they?" Val turned at the familiar voice. It took her a moment for the face to register.

"Barb?" She was towering over Val in a green floral dress, a white cardigan draped over her broad shoulders. Her wispy hair hung down and...was that lipstick? This chick was basically unrecognizable.

"What, you think I live at the diner?" She spread her arms wide. "I also enjoy culture."

"Yeah," Val said, a bit flummoxed.

"Haven't seen you around lately. Everything okay?"

"Yeah. Actually, things are pretty good," Val said. "Wait, did you miss me?"

Barb put a hand on her hip and eyed her in that familiar way. "Right, you're just a ray of sunshine."

A baby erupted into giggles nearby, crawling toward Val at lightning speed. "Oh, no, you don't," Barb said, bending down and scooping the child up. She flung the baby overhead and blew raspberries into their cheek, causing another peal of laughter. The type of laughter that sparked everyone in a ten-foot radius to smile involuntarily.

"Val, this is my grandbaby, Avery," Barb said, beaming with pride.

Val reached up and let Avery's tiny baby hand grasp her finger. The baby's hands were sticky, and her fierce grip forced all the blood to pool at Val's fingertip. Drool formed a line down her shirt, and she flashed Val a gummy smile, turning Val's insides to mush.

"I've got to get this little one back to her mother," Barb said.

Val freed her finger from the death grip and wiped her hand on her jeans. Barb smiled, her face so full of joy, Val thought her own heart might explode.

"See you at the diner soon?"

Val could only nod. Well, if Barb could repair her relationship with her daughter, there was hope for everyone else. She blinked rapidly to keep the tears at bay. Jesus, when did she become such a softie?

"Hey."

Val spun around to find Gina standing behind her, two beers in hand. Her forest green sleeveless shirt matched her eyes, and her well-defined biceps popped, whether from hauling kegs of beer around the bar or bench pressing small women, it was unclear. But Val secretly hoped for the latter.

Gina handed her a cup. "I saw you standing here empty-handed."

"Thanks." Val brought it to her lips, trying to hide the embarrassment that crept into her cheeks from the thought of becoming Gina's barbell.

"I'm glad you finally called," Gina said, tucking a strand of hair behind her ear.

The corner of Val's lips twitched uncontrollably. "Me too." A sound check from the stage crackled through the speakers, saving them from any more awkwardness. "Want to get closer?"

Gina nodded, and they weaved their way through a sea of people until they made it close enough to the stage.

"I brought a blanket if you don't mind sitting on the ground," Val said, nodding to the bag over her shoulder.

Without a word, Gina set her beer down, took the basket from Val's hands, and gently pulled the strap off her shoulder, leaving a trail of electric sparks where she grazed Val's arm. A flurry of fireworks shot off in her belly, and she was suddenly a teenager again, all gangly limbs and embarrassing hormones.

"Um..." Gina leaned over and pointed toward the food trucks. "Looks like you've got a fan."

Val followed her gaze, expecting to see Layla or Peter at the taco truck. But instead, Maddie stood waving her hands excitedly, a lemon-yellow sundress dancing about her knees. She flashed Val two thumbs-up, and Val couldn't help the goofy smile on her face.

"Oh, Maddie?" Val waved in her direction before turning back to Gina. "She's my personal cheerleader. Follows me everywhere I go, just to remind me how awesome I am." She exaggerated a flick of her ponytail, and Gina barked out a laugh.

Gina spread the blanket on the ground, and they took a seat.

"Well," Gina said after a moment. "I think everyone should have a personal cheerleader. I just hope she doesn't follow you everywhere." She nudged the toe of Val's shoe with her sandal, a playful look in her eye.

Val's stomach completed a roundoff and stuck the landing with a full set of jazz hands. But she didn't have time to contemplate what that meant because the chords of Van Morrison's *Brown Eyed Girl* crackled over the speakers.

Rupa shimmied her shoulders and danced across the stage before tossing a wink in Val's direction. Val couldn't help the smile that pulled on her lips. She didn't have one personal cheerleader, she had an entire cheering section. Val wasn't alone, she never had been.

She sneaked a glance at Gina who gave her a sly smirk, causing her insides to rock against her chest. At this moment, no one was rooting more for Val than herself. And this time, she wasn't faking it.

The End

Acknowledgments

When I first started writing, I had no idea how many people were involved in the process of creating a book. Turns out, a lot! I absolutely could not have gotten this far without Writing Mastery Academy. They not only continuously provide tools for my writing journey, but also introduced me to my cherished writing group: Camille Metcalf and Rita Potter. These two authors help me upcycle my blocks of word garbage into something comprehensible and cheer me on when I'm riding the struggle bus. Rita, especially, has played a big role in turning my writing around. Her patient tutelage and sound advice has guided me through both the writing and publishing process. I've learned so much from her!

I'm grateful to my editor, Tara Young, for reining in my errant use of commas and polishing this bad boy to make it shine. Thank you to Robyn Boettner and Kamakshi Sachidanandam for providing invaluable feedback on this particular story and to Vica Etta-Henrietta Steel for not only reading my work and providing insight, but for our lovely chats about everything from writing and religion, to all things queer and joyful.

A huge heap of appreciation goes to my dear friend Ru Nataraj for not only lending me the use of her name, but for being my soundboard and constant source of encouragement of all things creative and dreamy. She inspires the hell out of me!

Thank you to my mom for supplying me with copious amounts of books growing up and always supporting me in every creative endeavor. To Sayda Atwood for giving me a kick-ass illustration for my cover.

A big thank you to my husband and kids for putting up with me and my ever-growing catalog of hobbies. And I'm sure I've shared my excitement about my stories and complained about the process to far too many people to list here. Thank you for your ear-holes, friends.

And lastly, I'm grateful to you, reader, for taking a chance on me and this story. It means the world to me!

About the Author

B efore dipping her toes into writing and story creation, Shalon Atwood spent the majority of her career in the non-profit sector, working for various organizations and managing large volunteer programs before realizing that she'd rather be alone...in her sweatpants. She now hides behind a computer screen in the comfort of her own home, putting all of her weird thoughts on paper, while desperately trying to get her shit together. *The Faker's Guide to Self-Improvement* is her debut novel.

Follow along with her very real, not at all fake writing journey at shalonatwood.com.

9 798230 331049